She'd been attracted to him from the first moment she saw him.

But watching him struggle to be a father to the girls went straight to her heart, multiplying her desire.

His hand came up and tucked a stray hair behind her ear. "Thanks for your help." He started to lower his head, then stopped himself and took a step away from her.

After saying goodbye to the girls, Toni paused at the front door.

"Try another housekeeper, Zach. Eventually the girls will realize that they can't run everyone off."

"I'll do it. And, Toni…" He paused, then whispered, "Good night."

As she drove home, Toni wondered what Zach had wanted to say. She wished she could as easily turn off the feelings that Zachary Knight ignited in he

Dear Reader,

Once again, we've rounded up the best romantic reading for you right here in Silhouette Intimate Moments. Start off with Maggie Shayne's *The Baddest Bride in Texas*, part of her top-selling miniseries THE TEXAS BRAND, and you'll see what I mean. Secrets, steam and romance…this book has everything.

And how many of you have been following that baby? A lot, I'll bet. And this month our FOLLOW THAT BABY cross-line miniseries concludes with *The Mercenary and the New Mom*, by Merline Lovelace. At last the baby's found—and there's romance in the air, as well.

If Western loving's your thing, we've got a trio of books to keep you happy. *Home Is Where the Cowboy Is*, by Doreen Roberts, launches a terrific new miniseries called RODEO MEN. THE SULLIVAN BROTHERS continue their wickedly sexy ways in *Heartbreak Ranch*, by Kylie Brant. And Cheryl Biggs's *The Cowboy She Never Forgot*—a book *you'll* find totally memorable—sports our WAY OUT WEST flash. Then complete your month's reading with *Suddenly a Family*, by Leann Harris. This FAMILIES ARE FOREVER title features an adorable set of twins, their delicious dad and the woman who captures all three of their hearts.

Enjoy them all—then come back next month for six more wonderful Intimate Moments novels, the most exciting romantic reading around.

Yours,

Leslie J. Wainger
Executive Senior Editor

Please address questions and book requests to:
Silhouette Reader Service
U.S.: 3010 Walden Ave., P.O. Box 1325, Buffalo, NY 14269
Canadian: P.O. Box 609, Fort Erie, Ont. L2A 5X3

SUDDENLY A FAMILY

LEANN HARRIS

Silhouette®

INTIMATE™MOMENTS®

Published by Silhouette Books

America's Publisher of Contemporary Romance

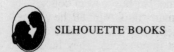 SILHOUETTE BOOKS

ISBN 0-373-07912-5

SUDDENLY A FAMILY

Books by Leann Harris

LEANN HARRIS

When Leann Harris first met her husband in college, she never dreamed she would marry him. After all, he was getting a Ph.D. in the one science she'd managed to avoid—physics! So much for first impressions. They have been happily married for over twenty years. After graduating from the University of Texas at Austin, Leann taught math and science to deaf high school students until the birth of her first child. It wasn't until her youngest child started school that Leann decided to fulfill a lifelong dream, and began writing. She presently lives in Plano, Texas, with her husband and two children.

I would like to thank the following people
for their help on this book:

Theresa McKinley Zumwalt, for her help on oil wells
and how things work in the oil fields
Eileen Wilks, for her knowledge of Midland
Jennifer Harrison, for her keen insight

Prologue

Zachary Knight looked up from the theft report he was studying, pinched the bridge of his nose, then ran his hand through his thick black hair.

"Damn," he growled. This was the third "incident" that had occurred over the last six months. As head of security for Anderson Oil, it was his responsibility to guard against this very thing. At the moment, he was doing a rotten job. Standing, he walked to the window and looked out at the flat, treeless horizon.

The phone rang, shaking him out of his dark thoughts. He walked back to his desk.

"Hello." The greeting sounded more like a curse; there was nothing cordial about it.

"Is this Zachary Knight?" the woman at the other end of the connection asked.

"Yes."

"My name is Charlotte Myers. I'm a social worker for the city of Phoenix. I have bad news for you. Your ex-wife was killed in a car accident. But I want to assure you your twin daughters survived the accident. Although Lori does have a broken leg, that was the only injury either child sustained. You will need to fly to Phoenix immediately and pick up the children.''

"Ms. Myers, are you sure you have the right man?" Zach asked, stunned by the woman's speech.

"You are Zachary Knight from Rio, Texas?"

"Yes," he replied. "But I've been divorced for close to five years."

"Your ex-wife was Sylvia Burton?"

His green eyes narrowed. "Yes."

"And you were married in Long Beach on February 5, seven years ago?"

"That's when the deed was done. But I don't know anything about children. When Sylvia and I separated, there weren't any children." That was the reason he left when he had. There had been no love left in the marriage, and Zach had vowed he wouldn't raise any kids in the same manner as he had been.

"Well, you are named on the girls' birth certificates as the father. Since we have located you, we would prefer to place the girls with their biological parent rather than with a foster family. We're swamped."

Zach's mind groped with the problem. "How old did you say the girls were?"

"About four and a half."

"What's the date of birth?" Zach asked.

"Let me see…they were born November 20, but it says here the girls were premature by eight weeks."

November 20. He had left on a Special Forces mission in mid-April. Seven months before the girls were born. It could be possible. When he and Sylvia had separated, their relationship—what relationship? That last week they had been together, they had either been yelling at each other or not speaking. But they had made love—no, that wasn't it.

They had had sex.

"Mr. Knight, can you come and pick up Lisa and Lori?"

It was a mistake. They couldn't be his. But he couldn't ignore them. His past made that impossible.

"I'll make arrangements to fly out this afternoon. Give me the address of where I can find you."

She did.

"We'll need for you to give a blood sample so we can check it against the children's. Also, I'll need some references from your current employer as to your character."

"I can supply that."

When he hung up, he stared at the phone. There had to be a mistake. He couldn't be a father. Sylvia wouldn't have done that to him, to keep his daughters a secret. Could she? He had a sick feeling in the pit of his stomach that she had. He'd go to Phoenix and straighten everything out. Then he would come back and catch the ring of thieves.

Chapter 1

Antonia "Toni" Anderson stepped off the elevator and froze. The sound of crying—children crying—floated down the hall. She glanced down at her father's golden retriever, Sam, which she was bringing back to her dad after she'd taken him to the vet. She noticed that Sam was on alert.

"I wonder who's got their kids here," she told the dog. His dark eyes met hers, and he whined.

As she walked down the hall, Toni searched for the source of the unusual sound. Here at the headquarters of her father's oil firm, in the hall that led to the executive offices, crying children weren't often heard. As a matter of fact, never heard. She remembered when she was small, her mother had always emphasized that she was to be on her best behavior.

The sound of distress drew her to the office midway down the hall. She didn't need to glance at the sign beside the door. That office belonged to Zachary

Knight, the head of security for the firm. Often, when she had walked to her dad's office, Toni glanced inside this office, wanting to catch a glimpse of the handsome, enigmatic man.

Zach's dark hair and green eyes were like a magnet, attracting females by the dozens. But the coldness in his eyes put most of the women off.

She peeked into the office. Zach's secretary was nowhere to be seen. Instead, the sight that greeted Toni made her stop and stare in stunned amazement. Zachary Knight knelt on one knee, his arms corralling identical twin girls, who were definitely unhappy.

"I don't want to be here," one little girl wailed. "I want my momma."

The other child didn't say anything, but from the expression on her face, she echoed her sister's sentiment.

"A doggy," one of the girls shouted. Zach released her and she ran to Sam. "Can I touch him?" Her eyes begged Toni for permission.

"Sure. Sam would love the attention." Toni showed the child how to stroke the dog's head. When she glanced up, the other twin, whose leg was in a cast, looked longingly at the dog. "Would you like to pet him, too?"

She nodded her head. Toni held out her hand and helped the child step close and guided her as she petted Sam.

Zach stood. A light of desperation shone in his eyes, one that she'd never seen before. "Toni, I want you to meet my twin daughters, Lisa—" he touched one twin "—and Lori." He moved his hand to rest on the injured girl's head.

Toni smiled at them.

Zach stepped closer and whispered, "I have a small problem here that I could use your help with." He looked at the girls.

His deep, rich voice played over her skin like a caress. This man was trouble, and she wanted to stay away from him at all possible costs.

"Isn't your secretary here?" Toni answered, looking around, praying to find the woman.

"I've just come back into town and found the office empty."

"Maybe Dad's secretary knows where she is. I'll go get her."

"No," he said, reaching out and grasping her by the elbow. Sparks of awareness shot through her. Apparently, the electricity was strong enough that he felt it, too, and he let her go. He cleared his throat. "I don't need help with anything connected with the company. I just need some advice."

Folding her arms under her breasts, Toni waited for his explanation.

"I'm tired," Lori said. The cherub had dark hair that had unraveled from her pigtails. The air of weariness about the child spoke of her distress. But what really touched Toni was the sight of a cast on the girl's right leg from below the knee down to her ankle.

Toni moved to the little girl's side and squatted down. "Do you need to sit down, Lori?" Toni asked.

Relief welled in her eyes. "Yes."

Without thinking, Toni scooped the girl into her arms and walked to the couch pushed against the far wall. She heard Zach pick up the crutches and follow. Sam, also, moved closer.

"Are you girls thirsty?" she asked the twins.

The question brought a light to their eyes and they nodded.

"I think I know where I could get you both a soft drink. And maybe some popcorn. Would you like that?"

Her question brought smiles to the girls' faces and they nodded.

"Okay, you wait here with Sam, and I'll be gone for a couple of minutes."

She headed down the hall to the small lunchroom beside her father's office.

"I'm going to help," Toni heard Zach tell the girls. Instantly, he appeared beside her, opening the door to the small kitchen.

Toni didn't say anything. The man had followed her for a reason. He'd get around to telling her in his own sweet time. She put the bag of popcorn into the microwave, then pressed the time button.

"I need your help, Toni."

Those were words that brought all sorts of images to mind. Thoughts of loving and wanting. But she knew that that wasn't what Zach had in mind.

"I need help with the girls. I'm lost here. If it was a fight, or terrorists or a kidnapping, I'd know how to handle things. But this—this—" He ran his hand through his short black hair. "I'm out of my element here."

He towered over her five-foot-five frame by a good six inches, and had the physique of a top-notch soldier, which he had been. There wasn't an ounce of spare flesh on him.

Think about the situation, Toni, and not about the man's assets, she chided herself.

"Can't the girls' mother help you?" Toni remembered Lisa asking about her mother.

His green eyes hardened. "My ex-wife was killed in a car accident. That's how Lori broke her leg."

That certainly answered several of her questions. He'd been married. But he'd left his wife to deal with twins alone.

Her face must have reflected her thoughts, because he said, "I didn't know about the girls until two days ago when I got a call from a social worker in Phoenix. Sylvia never told me she was pregnant. I guess she hated me enough to keep it a secret."

The timer on the microwave went off. Toni welcomed the distraction and pulled the bag from the interior. "Why don't you get a couple of drinks from the machine there?" She nodded to the vending machine in the corner of the room.

He pulled several coins from his pocket. "I need your help, Toni," he said again. "Suddenly, I've found myself in a situation where I have no experience. I'm drowning."

"What exactly are you asking, Zach?"

He put the coins into the machine and made his selection. After the cans rolled out, he turned and faced her. "Some temporary backup. On the flight, Lisa had to go to the rest room. I couldn't fit in there with her and she didn't want to go by herself. The stewardess saw the problem and helped. But—" he looked away "—all I need is help—"

The enormity of his request hit her.

"—for the evening. I need some frame of reference from which to operate." He sounded as if he were going into combat and not likely to return.

"C'mon, Zach. You can't tell me you don't remember how your father handled you."

"I was a bastard." The harsh edge to his voice said more about the situation than his words. "My father knew I existed and ignored me. My mother wasn't much better."

That cut the legs out from any argument she could think of. Still...

He took a step toward her. "You owe, me, lady," he said, his eyes narrowing, his voice hard.

"How do you figure that?" she demanded, annoyed at his attempt to strong-arm her.

"Carl Ormand."

The name hung in the air between them, evoking bitter memories of how Carl Ormand, an executive in her father's firm, had cornered her at a party last Christmas, convinced that she wanted him. When Toni tried to talk herself out of the situation, Carl hadn't listened and put his hands on her. She'd tried to get away but hadn't succeeded, and then Zach had stepped into the fray. He had dispatched Carl with a swift blow. Then Zach had followed her home and escorted her to the front door. When she had lifted her lips to his, he'd merely said good-night and walked away. Zach had never traded in on that incident until now.

She gazed into his eyes. The attraction that had sparked between them back then was still there, but neither of them had acted on it. When she had come back to Midland to teach at the University of Texas, she made it a point to avoid Zach. And had up to this point. But she owed him.

"All right. You get your wish. I'll help tonight."

He nodded, seemingly satisfied with her capitulation. Grinding her teeth, she comforted herself with the fact that his manipulation wasn't the reason she agreed to help. She knew that she couldn't have walked away from Lori and her injury. Not when she'd experienced firsthand the horror and pain of being hurt in a car accident years ago. But she didn't need to tell him that. Let him think what he will. She knew the real reason behind her actions.

Liar, a voice in her head whispered.

Zach breathed a sigh of relief at Toni's surrender. He was at his wits' end, feeling completely lost and woefully inadequate to handle this situation. How did one deal with four-year-old twin girls? He might have been able to cope with a single boy, but girls? What did he know about females? Hadn't Sylvia shown him how pathetically ignorant he was about how to treat the opposite sex? If he couldn't cope with a twenty-five-year-old woman, what made him think he could deal with four-year-olds? He ought to have his head examined.

When he flew to Phoenix, he was sure that there had been some mistake. Maybe Sylvia had listed him as the father simply to get back at him. They had not parted under the best of circumstances. Hah! They had parted as intimate strangers. But the instant he'd seen the children, he knew they were his. They looked exactly like the picture he had of his mother when she had been that age.

His mind had turned over the problem from a thousand different angles while they had been on the plane, and the only thing that had occurred to him is that he didn't know a single thing about preschoolers.

The situation hadn't improved after they landed in Midland. The girls had looked around the airport and

then at him and asked, "Where are the mountains?"
In Phoenix, the Superstition Mountains were in the distance, visible to all in the city. Here in Midland there were miles and miles of flat horizon.

He'd driven to the office first, wanting to check in with his secretary. At least that was what he told himself. What he had secretly hoped was that Nancy would have a useful suggestion on how to handle the situation. Maybe she would help. When he discovered she'd reported in sick for two days, he'd been desperate. Frowning over the problems, he'd looked at the girls and they had burst into tears, calling for their mother. He supposed it was the expression on his face that had scared them. He'd been known to put more than one Marine on edge with just a glance, so the girls' reaction wasn't so unexpected.

And then, like an angel sent from heaven, Toni had appeared in the doorway to his office with the dog, and the girls, literally speaking, had run to her. With a blinding insight, he knew she was the answer to his dilemma. No matter that he felt a definite sexual pull toward the woman and on more than one occasion had passionate thoughts about her. From the actions of his daughters, who were clinging to Toni like a lifeline, he knew he'd found help.

"Are you coming back?" a small voice from the door of the snack room asked, snapping him back to the present.

Zach looked up and saw the twin without a broken leg—Lisa—in the doorway. There was a look of terror in her green eyes. It had been clear to Zach since he picked the girls up this morning that they didn't like being with him. Yet, the prospect of being deserted yet again probably frightened them more than being with him.

Toni held out the bag of popcorn. "Yes, sweetie. Your dad and I were getting the popcorn and drinks for you. Why don't we go back and share this with your sister?"

Lisa looked at Toni, then at Zach, searching, he guessed, for the truth. Finally she nodded. "'Kay." She slipped her hand into Toni's.

Zach felt an odd settling in his chest, unlike anything he'd experienced before.

"Were you worried about us, Lisa?" Toni asked as they walked back to the office. Her voice, soft and mellow, made her question soothing.

"Naw." Lisa looked down, then at Toni. "But Lori was—you know, with her broke leg. Besides, you wouldn't leave Sam."

"Well, then, we should hurry back so Lori won't worry. Isn't that right, Zach?" Toni threw the question over her shoulder at him.

"Uh—right." He hadn't felt so awkward since he was fifteen and going through puberty, when his voice would drop an octave then shoot up like a bottle rocket.

When they entered his office, Lori sat on the couch, her fingers clutched in Sam's hair. The instant her sister entered the room, some of the fear left Lori's eyes.

"We're back," Lisa announced the obvious.

Zach was struck by the fact that these girls had lived with the uncertainty of not knowing what was going to happen to them after their mother's death. Of course, his being introduced to them as their father hadn't been a comforting experience. He was a stranger to them.

Lisa thrust out the bag of popcorn. "Want some?"

Lori took a handful. Zach held up the two cans of

soda. "I have a 7UP or a Dr Pepper. Which would you like?"

"The 7UP," Lori answered.

"I wanted that," Lisa complained. "I want the 7UP, please." Her eyes darkened with her entreaty.

"But this—" Zach held up the other drink "—is wonderful."

A militant look entered her eyes. Lisa folded her arms over her chest. "I want what Lori has."

Zach looked at Toni for help.

"I think you should go back and get another 7UP." She stepped closer. "You've just learned an important lesson. Buy two."

Zach shook his head and walked to the lunchroom for another drink. How was he to know all these little tricks?

When he stepped back into his office, the girls were greedily eating the popcorn. He popped the top and handed the drink to Lisa. She took a sip, then said, "I want the other drink."

Toni gave Lisa the Dr Pepper. Lisa sipped it, then smiled. "That's good."

Zach stared at the girls in disbelief. Lisa had just said she wanted a 7UP.

"When was the last time the children ate?" Toni asked Zach.

He didn't have any idea. "We had peanuts on the airplane." The girls hadn't complained, and he hadn't given food a thought.

Turning to the girls, Toni asked, "Did you have breakfast this morning?"

"Yeah, the lady that was taking care of us fed us oatmeal," Lisa answered. From the tone of her voice, it was clear that Lisa considered oatmeal to be an awful thing to serve to a child.

"I see." Toni's gaze met Zach's.

From the condemnation there, Zach felt about two inches tall. "I'm used to commanding soldiers in Special Forces. As I told you, I know nothing about—"

Toni held up her hand. "Why don't we go and have dinner?" She turned to the girls. "Do you two have a favorite place where you like to eat?"

Lisa and Lori looked at each other. "Yeah. We like Jerry's," Lisa said.

"What is Jerry's?" Toni asked.

"Pizza and clowns. It's fun," Lisa informed them.

Zach's eyes widened. Clowns and pizza? What in the world—?

Toni laid her hand on his forearm. "I have just the place for you. My big sister has a boy and girl, and they love to go to Pizza Charlie's. They have games and a yard with swings and slides." When Lori's eyes widened when she realized she couldn't participate, Toni added, "They have indoor games that you can play, too. You'll have fun."

Both girls smiled for the first time since Zach had picked them up this morning. A ray of hope penetrated the dark cloud hanging over his head.

Toni took the cans and empty bag from the girls and threw them away. "Okay, let me call my dad's office and have someone come and claim Sam, then we can go to Pizza Charlie's."

The girls nodded.

Toni moved to the desk and made the call. "Yeah, Betty, I'm in Zach's office and I have Sam with me. Will you send someone down to pick up the dog? Sure, no problem." Toni hung up. "Okay, we're all set."

Lisa looked at her. "Your daddy works here?" There was awe in her voice.

"He does." Toni threw a glance at Zach.

"And you've always had a daddy?" Lisa continued.

Zach winced. Damn, this pain was something new.

Toni didn't hesitate in her answer. "Yes, I've always had a daddy. But sometimes mommies and daddies can't stay together."

"Oh." Lori threw Zach a frown. Luckily George Anderson appeared in the doorway before she could ask any other questions.

"What's going on here?" he demanded.

Leaning down, Toni said in a stage whisper, "That's my dad."

Zach shook his head. The fat was in the fire now.

Chapter 2

"That's your daddy?" Lisa whispered in awe, her eyes round with wonder.

Smiling, Toni nodded and stood. "Hi, Dad. I was expecting Betty."

"I was leaving when you called."

Sam raced to George's side and gave his master a hearty greeting. After scratching the dog on the head, George pointedly looked at the girls. "What have we here?" His voice, which held a booming quality, made Lisa scoot to the edge of the sofa and reach for Toni.

Zach answered, "George, these are my daughters, Lori—" he nodded to the child on the sofa "—and Lisa." He pointed to the girl behind Toni.

"Well, you're a couple of mighty pretty girls. And I know about pretty girls. I had three of them." A frown gathered on George's forehead. "I don't recall you ever mentioning having children, Zach."

A muscle in Zach's jaw jumped. "I just flew in with

them today. Their mother was—'' He glanced at the girls and saw their distressed faces staring up at him. ''Toni's offered to help me with a few logistics.''

''Oh?'' Only George could make that single syllable sound so ominous.

''The girls are hungry, Dad, so will you take Sam home?''

George studied Toni, then Zach. There was a twinkle in his eye. ''Sure.''

Toni's instincts went on full alert. Something was going on behind that pleasant smile her father flashed her. But what? Since her mother had been killed last year, Toni had worried about her dad. He seemed so lifeless, so easygoing. Toni thought she'd never miss her dad's overbearing manner, but she had. Lately, he'd been showing signs of his old self, much to her relief.

Zach locked his office and they walked to the elevator. It took a long time with Lori hobbling on her crutches. As they stood waiting for the elevator, George smiled down at Lori. ''Did you know Toni spent a long time on crutches when she broke both of her legs?''

Lori shook her head. ''Did she have to use crutches, too?''

George looked at his daughter. ''She sure did. And for a long time she was in a wheelchair, too.''

Lori smiled shyly at Toni.

The elevator doors slid open and Zach handed the crutches to Toni and scooped Lori into his arms and walked on. Lori didn't look happy at the situation.

''This elevator is fast,'' Zach told Lori as he stepped into the interior.

Toni knew Zach was right. More than once she had

had to run to catch it. She smiled at the other twin. "Let's hurry."

The little girl grinned and raced into the elevator. George and Sam followed.

The car stopped on the eighth floor, and Carl Ormand stepped on. He smiled tightly at the crowd, though a growl from Sam took his smile away.

George and Carl exchanged a glance. "Leaving already, Carl?"

"I need to go out to one of the oil fields and check with the foreman about several pump jacks."

Toni bet Carl wouldn't know a pump jack if it bit him in the rear. But she refrained from saying anything. Zach caught her eye and she saw that he shared her opinion. Her dad had quit pushing Carl at her, for which Toni was very grateful. She wondered if Zach had ever told her father what happened at last year's Christmas party. No, she didn't think he had, because George would've fired Carl. Toni had never told her father about the incident because it had been so soon after the accident that had killed her mother. She hadn't wanted to disturb her father with Carl's obnoxious actions, so she kept quiet.

"I didn't know we'd branched out and started caring for kids here at the office," Carl said, sounding obnoxious and patronizing.

Zach's eyes narrowed. Lori, who was in his arms, visibly tensed. The girls didn't need this confrontation, Toni thought. As Zach opened his mouth, Toni touched his elbow and silently pleaded with him to avoid a fight.

"Don't make a fool of yourself, Carl," George snapped. "And if you're going to next comment about *my* dog, I suggest you don't."

Wisely, Carl didn't say anything.

When the elevator stopped at the ground floor, Carl raced out of the elevator ahead of everyone.

"I'll talk to you later, Dad," Toni said as she followed Lisa into the lobby.

"Have a good meal, and thanks for picking up Sam at the vet for me."

Toni had to grin. "It was nothing, Dad." She and her dad had been through a lot over the past ten years. Maybe they were on the other side of their troubles with each other. She kissed his cheek and winked.

"Can we go with you?" Lisa asked Toni.

Toni chanced a glance at Zach. Silently, she asked if that was okay.

"Of course."

All three females smiled. Zach looked disgruntled at their smiles.

"Where's your car?" Zach asked.

"Straight ahead. It's the red Jeep."

"Thanks for your help," he said as he walked beside her through the parking lot. The dark gruffness of his voice washed over her.

Lifting a shoulder, she tried to appear casual. "I owed you."

He nodded.

She stopped by the Jeep and opened the passenger-side door. While Zach buckled Lori into the front seat, Toni opened the back door for the other girl.

"Be sure and put on your seat belt, Lisa," she admonished. Toni waited until Zach finished and closed the door. "Do you know where the pizza place is located?"

"I've seen it a couple of times. It's on—"

"Why don't you follow me?" Toni held her breath

and waited for Zach's reply, wanting to know how he would react. Would he allow her to lead, or did he have to be the "man" at all times?

"Sounds good to me."

A smile broke across her face. His mouth started to turn up at he corners, then suddenly, it was as if a shutter came down across his face, and all emotion fled his face.

"I'm parked a couple of rows over. I'll drive over here."

As he walked away, Toni wondered about his reaction. Why had he decided that smiling was out of the question?

Zach raced to his 280ZX. It had been a nightmare getting the girls into it when they came back from Phoenix. When he looked at the car, then at the children, he only had his worst fears confirmed. He was not prepared for this experience.

He drove over to where Toni's car was parked. She headed out of the parking lot, with him following close behind her.

George's reaction worried him. The older man had a razor sharp mind. Zach didn't believe for a minute that George coming to his office was simply an accident. George had a reason for everything he did. Was George worried about him using Toni? Zach could understand the older man's view.

Gratitude filled Zach's heart when Toni had tempered his reaction to Carl. He had a few choice words for the fair-haired man, but they were things that his girls didn't need to hear. And again, he was struck by the fact that he wasn't prepared to be an instant father.

Maybe if he'd had a running start at it, he'd have a better chance.

He shook off the regrets. What good did it do now, wishing things could be different? All anyone could do was deal with the here and now. It had been a hard lesson to learn, but he had. And he wasn't going to ignore what he knew to be true.

And to add to the mixture, when Toni had smiled at him, it hit him square in the gut. He'd caught himself grinning back at her, like a teenager with his first crush. He'd managed to tamp down those reactions. He just hoped he could continue to do so.

"Was my daddy mad at your daddy?" Lisa asked Toni, leaning forward in her seat.

It appeared that of the two girls, Lisa was the chatty one. Toni wondered if the accident had changed Lori or if Lisa had always been the most extroverted of the two.

Toni glanced in the rearview mirror. Lisa appeared worried.

"No, I don't think so. Zach—your daddy—sometimes doesn't smile a lot."

"Yeah, we noticed," Lisa grumbled, folding her arms over her chest and flopping back against the seat.

Toni glanced at Lori beside her, and Lori agreed with her sister's assessment. Laughter bubbled up, and Toni chuckled. Both girls stared at her.

"I noticed it, too," Toni confided. "Maybe now that you two are with him, he will have a reason to smile more. I know my dad always loved to laugh with me and my sisters."

The girls looked at her, doubt coloring in their eyes.

"You don't believe me?" Toni asked.

Lori shrugged her shoulders. "Don't know. We haven't had a daddy before. He seems strange."

"And he doesn't smile," Lisa stated again. Apparently, that aspect of Zach worried Lisa.

How could she help these precious children understand what she didn't? Zach had always been a mystery to her, but a mystery that attracted her. He seemed far removed from her everyday world. She couldn't ever recall seeing him smile. How could she reassure the girls that their father had a lighter side when she'd never seen evidence of it herself?

"Well, I think that he was sad that your mother went to heaven."

"Mom said he didn't want us," Lisa commented.

Glancing in the rearview mirror, Toni looked at the little girl, hoping she heard wrong. From Lisa's bleak expression, Toni knew she hadn't.

"I don't think your daddy knew about you two girls," Toni explained, as she pulled into the parking lot of the pizza parlor.

Lisa frowned. "How come he didn't know?"

Toni was caught between a rock and a hard place. If she told them what Zach had shared, it would put their mother in a bad light. And yet telling them the truth was going to be hard.

"We're here at the pizza place," she said, hoping to divert the girls from the question. "What kind of pizza do you like the best?" she asked Lori.

"I like meat on my pizza."

Zach appeared at the passenger-side door and opened it. He reached for Lori, but she frowned. Toni noticed the girl's reaction. Leaning over the steering wheel, she looked at Zach. "Maybe Lori would like to walk. Why don't you ask her?"

The idea of asking the child her opinion seemed to startle Zach. Then he shrugged. "Do you want to walk, Lori?"

She thrust out her chin. "Yes."

Zach stepped back and held the crutches for Lori as she wiggled out of the car. As she watched Zach help Lori, Toni was pleased that Zach had followed her advice. Maybe there was hope in this situation after all.

Zach set down his tea glass, then followed Toni's gaze to where Lori played Skee Ball. She tossed the wooden ball and hit the bull's-eye.

"It seems Lori is very good at that," Toni commented. Lori stood on her good leg and tossed another ball at the bull's-eye.

Lisa was on the other side of the room, watching the singing, robotic bear.

Toni wondered if she should let Zach know what the girls had said about him.

"You're itching to say something." He turned to her. "What is it?"

Her startled gaze flew to his. "How—?"

"It's written on your face. You wouldn't make a good operative in a covert operation. You're easier to read than a kid's book."

Her brow arched. "On the drive over here the girls asked why you didn't know about them. I didn't answer them."

"I already told you that their mother never thought it necessary to tell me." His bitterness rang clearly in his voice.

"Yes, but I couldn't tell them that their recently departed mother lied to them to get back at you."

"Why not?"

"Don't be ridiculous. What would be served by telling them that? They've had enough trauma in the past few weeks. Adding to it won't help things."

"Then what did you tell them?"

He hit the nail on the head. "Uh—I didn't say anything. But I think we need to come up with some story to tell."

"You'll have to come up with it. They didn't cover storytelling in Special Forces training, nor was it in the field training course we had." He looked back at the girls.

"How about being a pain in the b—" Toni bit off the end of the word.

Zach's head whipped around and he pinned her with a sharp gaze. One corner of his mouth kicked up. "*That* was included in the training. And I excelled at it."

"I don't doubt it."

He grinned.

Disgruntled that he had pushed her into mudslinging, she looked at the girls. What was a good reason to give them for their mother not telling Zach about them?

"We can tell them the truth," she commented, deciding her mother's motto of always telling the truth would serve her well in this instance.

"You want to tell them that their mother couldn't stand the sight of me and refused to talk to me that last day?" Disbelief filled his voice.

"No, of course not. But the closer we stick to the facts, the better off we'll be."

He waited for her to continue.

"We'll tell them that their mom was mad at you."

"An understatement," he grumbled.

Ignoring his comment, she went on. "We'll tell them

that because their mother was mad at you, she decided not to tell you about the girls. They can relate to being mad at someone and not telling them everything. We don't have to throw stones at her, but simply state the truth. I think the girls will buy that explanation. Then you can tell them that as soon as you discovered their existence, you came.''

Apparently, her argument was gaining ground with him. "You might have a point." He rubbed the back of his neck. His hands were strong and sturdy.

There was a long scar across the back of his right hand. She wondered how he got it.

"So, when are you going to tell them this story?" Zach asked.

His question startled her out of her thoughts about him. She felt her face heat with embarrassment.

"We did decide to tell the girls why I didn't know about them, didn't we? Or did I miss something?" He looked truly puzzled.

It was becoming clearer and clearer that Zach might be an expert in the field of security, probably knew a dozen ways to incapacitate a man, but he didn't know zip about children.

"Yes, we did. And if they ask again, you need to answer them. Or if they ask me, I'll answer them, but just blurting it out isn't a good idea. The rule with children is when they ask a question, you answer it in the easiest, simplest way you can. If they want to know why the sky is blue, you can say 'God made it that way.' You really don't need to give them the physics of the situation.''

His brow arched. "And do you know why the sky is blue?"

"Yes. It's because, in air, the scattering cross section

for blue light is greater than for red light.'' She'd suffered through her college physics class and this was the
first time she had been able to use some of the information she'd learned. ''I could go on to explain more
about the frequency and the fourth power, but I think
that would probably be too much for the purpose of
this discussion.''

He scowled at her, not appreciating her point.

Toni glanced at the twins and noticed that Lori was
resting on her crutches. ''I think maybe it's time to
take Lori home. She's showing signs of fatigue.''

Zach glanced at Lori, who sagged against her
crutches. He laid a twenty on the table to pay for their
dinner. ''I'll get Lori if you'll go get her sister.''

''Divide and conquer. I can deal with that. Oh, and
Zach,'' she added, ''smile for the girls. Lisa noticed
you don't smile. It worried her.''

He gaped at her.

''Their world's been turned upside down,'' Toni
hastily explained. ''A friendly smile will help them to
cope with the situation.''

There was a considering light in his eyes, before he
turned and walked to Lori.

Toni retrieved Lisa from the singing bear and led her
to where Zach held the other girl in his arms.

''We'll still need to use your car,'' Zach said as they
walked out of the restaurant. ''I guess I'll have to get
something bigger for everyone.''

''Get a car like Toni's,'' Lisa informed him. ''She's
got the right kind of car.''

Zach looked at Toni. It was one more thing that
would have to change in his life. But from the determined light in his eye, Toni knew he would do it.

His resolve was admirable. Too bad it attracted her.

* * *

Toni and the girls stood motionless as Zach closed the door on his efficiency apartment. The place was quite unbelievable. The little space had a semikitchen with a small refrigerator, a hot plate and sink. There was a couch, a stuffed chair and a small wooden table with four chairs.

"It's not much," Zach offered by way of explanation, as he set the suitcases on the floor.

The understatement didn't need a reply. Toni turned to him. "The girls can't possibly live here."

He ran his hand through his hair. "I know."

A wave of concern washed over Toni. Not only did Zach suddenly have a family, but his car and house were both going to have to be changed.

"The couch makes into a bed," he explained as the children looked around the room. "The bathroom is through there."

Toni shrugged. She'd already protested the small space. They'd just have to make do tonight. "Why don't I help the girls get ready for bed while you make up the bed for them?"

He nodded, looking relieved that he wouldn't have to take up that gauntlet right now. She swallowed the smile that tried to surface. Whoever would have thought that an ex-Special Forces soldier would be rattled by the thought of bathing two four-year-olds?

After gathering nightgowns and toothbrushes from their suitcases, Toni led the girls to the bathroom. She filled the tub, and helped Lisa into the water. While she played, Toni gave Lori a sponge bath.

"Where's Daddy?" Lisa asked.

"He's making up your bed," Toni answered as she washed off the little body. Lori sat on the closed toilet.

A puzzled frown gathered on Lori's brow. "Where is our bed?"

"Your daddy said the couch makes into a bed."

"Where's Daddy going to sleep?" Lisa asked.

Toni looked down into the solemn little face. "I'm not sure. But don't you worry about it. Things are going to work out."

Neither girl looked convinced.

"Let's get you out of the tub and brush your teeth. I bet it has been a long day."

The girls looked at each other. Toni could only guess at the silent communication going on between them. They hurriedly finished, put on nightgowns and panties Toni had taken from their suitcases, then went back into the living room. Zach had pulled out the bed and it looked inviting.

"It looks like your dad has your bed ready. Why don't you two get under the covers?"

Lisa scampered and Lori hobbled to the bed. After they were tucked in, their little faces stared back at Toni. She knew the girls would need a final parting. "Why don't we say a good-night prayer so you can go to sleep?"

"We don't know one," Lisa informed her.

"Well, then I'll teach you the one my mother taught me."

Toni sat on the bed and said the simple prayer, then the girls repeated it. Impulsively, Toni leaned over and kissed each girl. Lisa threw her arms around Toni and squeezed.

"Your daddy will take good care of you."

"Why can't you stay?" Lisa asked plaintively. Her eyes beseeched her.

Toni swallowed and didn't venture a glance at Zach.

"Because, sweetie, I have a home of my own. Besides, there's not a bed for me."

"We can scrunch together."

The simple logic of children. "But where's your daddy going to sleep?" Toni asked.

They looked at their father. "He can sleep in the bed, too."

Sneaking a look over her shoulder, she saw Zach's face. He appeared surprised and stunned. His gaze met hers.

"Well, you asked," he softly replied.

Turning back to the girls, she said, "Your daddy and I would have to be married to do that."

"Okay," Lisa answered.

She had been neatly cornered by a four-year-old. What could she say?

"Your dad hasn't asked me." Toni thought she'd outmaneuvered the child.

Lisa looked at her father. "Do you want to marry Toni?"

Now she definitely didn't want to see Zach's expression. Toni grasped Lisa's hand. "Grown-ups are funny, sometimes. Getting married isn't as simple as your daddy asking me. We need to be in love."

"Why?" Lisa was tenacious and determined.

"It's a grown-up thing."

"Grown-up things are stinky." She folded her arms over her chest and tried to look stern.

Toni stared at the frightened faces of the two little girls. Although they didn't say anything more, she saw from their expressions that they didn't want to be left alone with Zach. She knew that Zach wasn't any happier than the girls about this situation. She grabbed her purse and moved to the door where Zach stood.

Toni glanced at the bed. "Where are you going to sleep?" Her gaze collided with his. That electricity that always seemed to be there flared.

"I can stretch out on the floor."

Toni looked at the carpeted room. "You sure?"

His brow arched. "I've spent nights in a lot worse situations than this. This is a piece of cake."

If this was a piece of cake, why did she feel as if she were deserting a sinking ship? "If you need anything, give me a call."

As she opened the door, Zach snagged her wrist. Her startled gaze met his.

"Thanks." The heat in his eyes made her swallow hard.

"You're welcome."

As she walked to her car, Toni wondered how Zach would make it with the girls. Theirs hadn't been a strong beginning.

Zach threw his pillow and blanket on the floor. Stretching out, he pulled the pillow under his head. This wasn't bad. It certainly ranked higher than a lot of places he'd slept.

Staring at the ceiling, Zach smiled as he thought about how Lisa tried to get Toni to stay and sleep with them.

There's not a bed for me.

We can scrunch together.

But where's your daddy going to sleep?

He can sleep in the bed, too.

Your daddy and I would have to be married to do that.

Okay.

Your dad hasn't asked me.

Do you want to marry Toni?

After Sylvia, his first wife, Zach had decided that he would never again marry for "love." He'd never be at the mercy of those feelings again. Life with Sylvia had been hell. After the initial blaze of lust had died between them, he and Sylvia had had nothing in common. They didn't even like the same kind of food. He loved Mexican, she had a thing for Chinese.

But having a wife would solve the majority of the problems he was facing.

Nope, he wasn't going to use the girls as an excuse to scratch the itch he had.

Zach wasn't exactly jumping up and down with joy about becoming a father, but he'd be dammed if he'd walk away from the children.

He knew firsthand the bitterness of having your father reject you. His dad had gotten his mother pregnant while he had been separated from his wife. When he learned she was pregnant, he told her too bad, that he was going back to his wife. His dad had never acknowledged him. When Zach had finally confronted the man, it had been a bitter meeting, and as Zach walked away from it, he had promised himself that he would never desert any child of his.

So, now he had two daughters. And no matter what it took, he was going to care for them.

He thought about Toni. She was a lovely woman— slender, with light brown hair that came down to her chin, soft blue eyes and a smile that tempted him to do more than just say thank you.

Admit it, a voice in his head whispered. *She gets to you.*

He ignored the taunt.

"Daddy?" a small voice from the bed called.

Sitting up, Zach looked at the bed. ''What?''

''I have to tinkle,'' Lori told him, a hesitation in her voice. She was going to need help getting to the bathroom.

''Okay.''

He wished Toni was still here.

Chapter 3

Toni glanced at the bedside clock. It was 5:00 a.m. She'd been awake for the last hour. Finally, she gave up the struggle to sleep. Slipping out of bed, Toni reached for her robe.

How was Zach coping with Lori and Lisa?

What could go wrong while everyone was asleep? she asked herself. She didn't know, but considering how things had been going for Zach lately, she wasn't going to be surprised by anything that happened.

Walking into the kitchen, she flipped on the light and set water on the stove for a cup of hot tea. Lisa's plea for Toni to stay with them had replayed itself over and over in her brain.

A yearning that Toni had been able to ignore over the past few years had sprung to life again. Children. She wanted children. She'd given up on men—or more specifically on finding the right man to marry. Toni didn't want a hard-driving man like her father, so when she had left home and gone to the University of Texas at Austin to teach ornithology, she had quickly gotten involved with a man whom she thought was the complete opposite of her father—sensitive and tender. Yeah, right. Mark turned out to be a jerk, who was sleeping with her best friend.

The whistle on the kettle sounded, and Toni poured the water over the tea bag. Although she tried to avoid the memory, the images popped into her head. She'd gone to Mark's apartment to drop off flowers and a cake to celebrate his birthday.

When she'd heard a sound from the bedroom, Toni went to investigate. She had planned to surprise Mark and had certainly done that when she saw Mark and Melissa in bed together. The memory still made her wince. She must've made a sound, because the couple on the bed stopped and looked at her.

Sipping her raspberry tea, Toni remembered her actions that day. She had dashed out of the bedroom, grabbed the cake off the kitchen table and when Mark came barreling out of the bedroom, she'd heaved it at him. He howled like a branded cow, but it was funny to see him wearing nothing but frosting.

From that moment on, Toni had given up the idea of finding a man to love. There didn't seem to be one worth the effort.

Besides, even if she found a good man, the doctors had told Toni the injuries she'd suffered when she was in the car accident had left scar tissue on her Fallopian tubes, and they didn't believe she'd ever conceive. She had missed the idea of children but thought she'd resolved the issue in her heart. The twins yesterday had revived that longing.

She gulped down the last sip of the tea. Too bad she

couldn't just be a mother to the girls, but she doubted Zach would rent out the children or give them to her every other weekend to satisfy her longings.

If he would, that might solve everyone's problem.

"I'm hungry, Daddy," Lisa complained in the morning.

It jarred Zach every time either child called him "Daddy." The first time Lisa murmured that word, it was as if a crack had appeared in the shell around his heart. Each time either girl repeated it, the crack widened.

"Me, too," Lori added. "I'm hungry."

"I want some Froot Loops," Lisa demand.

Zach learned early on that of the two girls, Lisa was the more vocal. Lori was the quieter one. He didn't know if she let Lisa take the lead because she was hurt, or if things had always been that way.

"Froot Loops?" he repeated. "Do you really like them?"

"It's my favorite," Lisa said. "And you have to have milk, too."

"And orange juice," Lori added.

"I've got water. And coffee."

"Ick," Lisa said.

From the looks in his children's eyes, coffee wasn't what they were wanting. Picking up the phone, he dialed the number that Toni gave him last night. When she picked up, he said, "What are Froot Loops?"

"Daddy, my stomach's making noises," Lisa complained.

"Are you having some problems?" Toni asked.

"They're talking in a language I don't know. I need a little help here," Zach shot back.

"Froot Loops is a cereal." She paused. "You want some help?"

"Anything you can do will be appreciated."

"I'll be there in a few minutes. Tell the girls I'm coming with the Froot Loops."

He hung up and turned to the twins. "Toni's coming with the cereal."

"Is she going to bring Sam?" Lori asked.

"I don't know." The questions they asked boggled his mind. What did a dog have to do with a breakfast cereal? How had they made that connection?

Zach could only be grateful that Toni was on her way.

A knock sounded at the door.

"Yippee, she's here." Lisa raced to the door.

Zach's sentiments were reflected in his daughter's response. Before he could take the chain off the door, Lisa tried to open it.

"Wait a minute, Lisa. I need to remove the chain."

"Hurry up," the child commanded as she danced around. "I'm hungry."

When he heard Toni's soft laugh, a shaft of heat raced through him. Stepping to the door, he slid the chain out of its track. The instant he did, Lisa pulled on the knob, throwing open the door.

"Toni," Lisa cried and ran to the woman and hugged her leg.

Zach felt like a man carrying the plague. Unwanted and unneeded.

Lisa looked up and noticed the sacks that Toni carried. "McDonald's? Did you go to McDonald's?"

She smiled. "Well, there is a big McDonald's by my

house and I thought you girls might like something from there instead of Froot Loops.''

Nodding vigorously, Lisa said, "Do I get pancakes? I love 'em. Lori likes the eggs. Do you have eggs?''

Toni smiled at Zach. There was laughter and joy in her eyes. "Good morning."

"Do you need help?'' he asked, pointing to the sacks.

"I left the coffee and orange juice in the car. Would you go get it?''

"You brought coffee?'' He couldn't keep the relief out of his voice. He wouldn't be forced to drink his old, tasteless instant in the cabinet.

Her grin widened. "I thought you might want a cup.''

"You're a mind reader.''

"Naw. I just remembered my dad wasn't too cheerful in the mornings until he had his coffee. I thought that you might need the caffeine this morning in particular.''

He hurried out to her car and gathered up the box with the drinks in it. By the time he got inside the apartment, the girls were digging into their food.

"There's another breakfast of scrambled eggs and sausage or an Egg McMuffin. Your choice.''

An odd feeling settled in Zach's chest. He couldn't quite identify it, but it felt good and he didn't question it. "I'll take the eggs.''

They joined the girls at the table. It was odd having every chair filled. Zach paused as he looked at the faces of his children. Then his gaze met Toni's. He tried to hide his feelings, but he had the oddest sense that she'd seen what was in his heart.

"How did the night go?" Toni asked, after swallowing a bite of her breakfast.

"Okay," Zach mumbled, glancing at Lori. He remembered the awkward moment when he helped her into the bathroom.

"No problems?"

She sounded surprised, which annoyed him. No matter that it was true. How could a four-year-old child jerk the rug out from under a Special Forces commander?

He didn't bother answering.

"Do you plan to go house hunting today?"

Zach glanced up from his breakfast. "I thought I might ask the manager if they have an apartment in the complex with two bedrooms."

"Oh."

He didn't like the sound of that. "What's wrong with that?"

"Well, I just thought you might like to raise the girls in a house."

"Yes, but I thought—"

The phone rang. He answered it immediately, wanting to give himself time to think of an answer to Toni's comment.

"Zach, this is Henry Watkins. We have a problem."

"What is it?" Zach shot back.

"There's been an accident. One of the drivers came to field number one to pick up a load of crude. He found the gauger dead at the bottom of a storage tank, and the tank from which he was to get his load was empty. We've got problems."

He was right. This time there was a dead body accompanying the missing oil. He looked at the table. All three females had stopped eating and were watching him.

"All right, Henry, I'll be right out."

"Okay. Do you want to call the boss?"

"Yeah, I'll contact him. Have you called the police?"

"Sure have. They're on the way."

"Good." Zach hung up the phone and ran his hand through his hair.

"What's wrong?" Toni had set her breakfast sandwich down and was intently watching him.

"There's been an accident in field number one."

"What kind?" Toni asked.

Her question shouldn't have surprised him, but it did. Toni knew the oil business.

He motioned for Toni to follow him into the kitchen. "One of the drivers found Wayne Thompson, the gauger, dead beside a reserve tank. I'm going to need to get out there after I talk to your dad." He noticed an understanding flare to life in her eyes.

"What happened to the gauger?"

"That's what we want to know."

Zach dialed George's home number and told him what had happened. "Yeah, I'll meet you at the site." Zach hung up.

The girls continued to stare at Zach. He lowered his voice. "I need to go, Toni," he whispered. "Do you think you could take care of the girls today?"

His eyes remained oddly flat, as if expecting her to refuse him, to disappoint him as others had done in the past.

Glancing over her shoulder at the girls, Toni saw their worried expressions as they stared back. Here were two little girls who needed her, and she couldn't turn her back on them. "All right, Zach. I'll keep the girls today."

His stance eased and a look of relief and surprise raced across his face. "I don't know how long I'll be."

"I understand." She grinned. "Remember who my father is."

"I guess you do. I wish there was another solution, but this is my responsibility, my job. I'm the head of security."

"Don't worry, Zach. The girls will be fine. I have a class to teach at one this afternoon, but the university has a day-care center on campus. I'm very friendly with the woman who runs it. There should be no problem with dropping the girls there for a while. When you get back, call me at home."

The girls gave her worried looks.

Toni returned to the table, leaned down, and whispered, "I think we could also pick up Sam and have him spend the afternoon with us."

Both children nodded with enthusiasm.

At the door, Zach turned back to Toni. "I'll try to get back as soon as possible." As he reached for the door, he looked over his shoulder. "Bye, girls. Toni will take care of you until I get back." Two cherubic faces nodded solemnly. He opened the door, but instead of leaving at once, Zach lingered, his gaze meeting Toni's. "Thanks for your help."

"No problem."

He nodded and softly closed the door.

Toni faced the girls. "I guess it's just us three, but we'll find something to fill our day."

Oddly enough, Lori and Lisa looked excited to be with her. Their response warmed Toni.

* * *

The scene at field number one was ordered chaos. The police had taped off the steel stairway above the body. The coroner took pictures, while the tanker driver watched.

Zach walked up to Henry Watkins, the field engineer, who was talking to the detective and the tanker driver. Henry introduced Zach.

The detective shook his hand. "Martin Phelps. I was questioning your driver here. He found the body."

"And what did he say?" Zach asked.

"He says when he drove up, he honked, waiting for the gauger to appear out of the foreman's shack, but no one answered him. So he drove his rig back to the tank. That's where he found the body. At the bottom of the reserve tank. About that time, Henry drove up."

Zach looked at the driver. "So, he was dead when you got here?"

"Yup. I didn't see anyone around here."

After talking to the police, Zach and Henry walked to the shack and went inside. They glanced around to see if everything was in order.

Henry looked at the top of the filing cabinet for the field's logbooks. "Zach, I don't see the logbooks." Henry pulled out each file drawer in the place, searching for the records.

After a thorough search, they turned up nothing.

"Is everything okay in here?" Martin asked, walking inside.

"No. We're missing the logbooks for this field." Zach wondered if Martin knew that the logs were the records of the field's weekly production, but the detective didn't ask for clarification.

The door to the shack opened again, and the driver stuck his head inside. "We've got a problem. I was supposed to pick up crude out of the number three tank in this field. Well, it's as dry as the prairie around here.''

Zach looked at Henry, then Martin. ''It seems as if we have another problem.''

''And maybe a motive for murder?'' Martin asked.

''Afraid so,'' Zach replied.

Zach turned off the engine of his car and leaned back to look at the peaceful house beyond the well-kept lawn. Toni's house. Inside were people waiting for him. That particular situation hadn't occurred in a long time.

He glanced at his watch. Nine. He'd spent the entire day at the field, looking for the logbooks, going to the gauger's house and searching it with Martin Phelps. They hadn't found the information.

What had been obvious from the moment he'd arrived at the scene was that something was out of kilter in that field. George had shown up asking questions about what had occurred. The empty reserve tank had either been drained by some unauthorized individual, or the pump jack had gone out in the field. George had ordered a check on the equipment.

Reaching for the door handle, Zach was reminded of the cut on his side. George had demanded that they drive to see about the pump jack leading to that field. After they'd seen it, they knew the jack had burned out, causing the reserve tank to go dry. As Zach had stepped away from the pump, a corner of the iron bracing caught him on the side, tearing his shirt and causing a long, bloody gash. George had told him to go to the doctor and get it cleaned up. But Zach had decided he needed to get back to the girls. He'd had worse scrapes on missions he'd gone on.

Once out of the car, Zach heard the dog inside the house barking. Before he could knock, Toni appeared at the door.

"You look tired," she said.

All sorts of fantasies raced through his brain—dangerous thoughts that he couldn't give in to. "It was a long day," he answered, stepping into the foyer. Sam greeted him; then, after obviously satisfying himself that Zach was no threat, the dog loped down the hall.

Looking around, Zach asked, "Where are the girls?"

"Asleep. If you want to follow Sam, he's in the room with Lisa and Lori."

Zach walked down the hall and looked into the room where the girls slept. The dog settled on the floor at the foot of the bed.

"Why don't you leave them there for the night? Lori was very tired, so I put both girls to bed. They went to sleep right away."

He didn't want to believe she cared about the girls. Yet, it was there in her gaze.

"They'll be all right tonight," she assured him.

"Yeah, you're right." When he turned to go, he heard Toni gasp.

"You're hurt, Zach."

"It's nothing."

She touched his arm. "Why don't you let me put something on it? You don't want it to get infected."

"It's nothing."

She gave him a dark look. "There's no reason for you to be macho about it. Let me take care of it. Besides, now you have two little girls depending on you, and you can't afford not to take care of yourself."

Zach couldn't remember the last time he'd been scolded about anything. He found it amusing. "Yes, ma'am."

Her eyes narrowed. "I've handled harder cases than you, Zachary Knight. After a lifetime of dealing with my dad, I believe I know how to handle your type."

"My type?"

"Pigheaded males."

He grinned. "Why don't you lead the way to where you want me?"

She walked to the bathroom and turned on the light. As Zach came toward her, she noticed that he limped slightly. When he saw the direction of her gaze, he softly said, "It's an old injury. It acts up now and then."

From her expression, Zach knew she wanted to question him about his limp. It was a touchy subject for him, the reason he'd left the military. He'd thought he'd dealt with it. But he knew he didn't want to talk about it. He gave her his best I-don't-want-to-talk look.

Pointing to the closed toilet seat, she said, "Take off your shirt and sit there."

He didn't argue; he simply obeyed. When he slipped off his shirt and laid it on the tub, her eyes widened. She stepped around him and gently cleaned the wound. Her touch was as light as a butterfly's, but oddly enough, Zach's body reacted violently to it. His mind wasn't concentrating on how the wound hurt. He had more basic thoughts consuming his brain.

"How did you do this?" she asked.

He explained.

"Why didn't you go to the doctor?"

He glanced over his shoulder. Her lips were inches

away, and he had the stupid urge to lean closer and cover her mouth with his. "It isn't bad."

Her brow shot up. "Only for you macho tough guys is it minor." Her sarcasm wasn't lost on him.

"I've gotten worse and had to continue."

"Ah, yes, that military thing." She squirted antibacterial ointment on the wound, then pulled a sterile pad out of a box and placed it on the cut.

"Do you have something against the military?" he asked.

Tearing off strips of tape, she shook her head. "Not a thing."

After she secured the pad, she stepped back. "That should take care of it." Her eyes met his and heat raced through his body. He wanted to reach out and pull her into his arms and kiss her.

She wet her lips and all the air left his lungs. Zach reached out and touched her chin with his fingertips.

"Thanks for taking care of that," he softly said. Temptation yawned before him.

The pupils of Toni's eyes dilated. "No problem."

He felt the heat of her breath brush over his thumb. Slowly, his hand came to rest on her neck. Every beat her heart took thundered through him.

He was going down in flames, and every instinct of self-preservation screamed at him to stop. Dropping his hand, he stood up, which only made the situation worse. His chest was inches from her breasts.

"I'll leave you to get dressed. Are you hungry? I've got some leftover chicken."

What he needed to do was get the hell out of here. "I'm fine."

She nodded and walked out of the room.

Zach took a deep breath. What had just happened?

Why had he suddenly lost all sense of reason and nearly jumped off the cliff again?

What he needed to do now was put on his shirt and get out of this house before his hormones overrode his good sense.

"Have you hidden the logbooks?"

"I've got them in a secure place." The man paced around the living room. "I don't know why you had to kill Wayne. He was a big help."

"He was turning chicken on us. Apparently, Zachary Knight had been nosing around, asking questions. Wayne wanted to stop stealing and lay low for a while. When I told him that things were under control, he didn't believe me. He didn't want to cooperate anymore. It was just a matter of time before he would have been spilling his guts and dragging us down with him. I couldn't let that happen."

"What if the cops discover he was killed?"

"I made it look like it was an accident. No one will ever know the difference."

Fear laced the man's eyes. "I hope you're right."

Chapter 4

Zach stopped at an all-night diner on his way home. What he really wanted was a good stiff belt of whiskey, but he needed to think clearly and alcohol wouldn't help. Coffee would.

The waitress showed him to a booth and asked if he needed anything to go with his coffee. Zach read the invitation in her eyes, but he wasn't interested.

"Just coffee," he replied.

The woman's smile disappeared, and she left. Within a minute, she returned with a cup and a pot of coffee. Zach nodded his thanks and picked up the drink. It tasted like they'd been soaking old shoes in the brew, but it was strong and filled with caffeine.

It appeared his entire life was going to hell with the speed of a rocket from a launcher. Smelling the fragrance of Toni's hair while she gently cleaned his side had been a worse torture than anything the terrorists in South America had dished out when he'd been caught helping George Anderson escape from his kidnappers. Zach had been prepared for their torture. But the soft scent that seemed to be so much a part of Toni had slipped under his guard, going straight into his heart. He'd been tempted to pull her into his arms and let his lips feast on hers.

And he wouldn't have wanted to stop there. But it was the strength of that reaction that had scared the fire out of him. The last time he'd felt anything remotely like that, he'd ended up married to the woman and living in hell for several years after. It was a mistake he didn't intend to repeat again. And since avoiding marriage had been a guiding force in his life these past few years, why all of a sudden had he forgotten it?

He took another gulp of the bitter brew.

Toni Anderson. A vision of her formed in his brain…her soft blue eyes, kissable mouth and rich reddish brown hair that curled around her face, making her look like a teenager. But her body, and his, testified that she was a full-grown woman.

He cursed. That's all he needed in addition to all the other changes in his life—a libido that was out of control. It was a feeling he didn't like.

It had been a hell of a day. First waking up to the girls peeking over the bed at him, their faces a combination of curiosity and worry. Lisa had wanted to wake him, but Lori had not supported the idea. He guessed the girls were still frightened of him.

The only thing that had saved his hide this morning was having Toni there when the call came in about the trouble in the oil field. What he needed to do was hire a housekeeper to be with the girls and take care of them if another emergency occurred. And he needed to find a bigger place to live.

But what he needed the most was to find out what really happened in field number one.

He pulled out his wallet and paid for the coffee.

As he drove home, he wished his reaction to Toni could be so easily dealt with as his housing problem.

As for what happened in field number one today, he'd get to the bottom of that mystery.

In the morning the girls' laughter rang through the house as they played with Sam.

"Throw the ball, Lori," Lisa admonished her sister. "I'll race Sam to get it."

Their laughter filled Toni with pure joy. A dream come true. Now if she only pressed her imagination a little, she could see a husband, who was tall, with brown hair and green eyes, who looked amazingly like—

Whoa! she chided herself. She didn't need the kind of grief that a strong man like Zachary Knight would bring to her life. She'd lived a lifetime with such a man, her dad, and wanted to avoid that trait in a husband, no matter how much he made her blood thunder.

Sam barked and Lisa giggled as they raced into the kitchen chasing the ball. Lisa slipped and fell at Toni's feet.

Leaning down, Toni helped the little girl to her feet. "You need to be careful, or you'll end up on crutches like Lori."

Toni saw the child blanch at her words. She hadn't meant to remind the girls of the accident that killed their mother. "Aw, sweetie, I'm sorry," Toni whispered, leaning down to hug Lisa.

"We miss Mom." Lisa's voice cut through Toni.

Glancing over Lisa's shoulder, Toni saw Lori stand-

ing frozen in the doorway, her expression as sorrowful
as her sister's. Guiding Lisa toward the other girl, Toni
hugged both of them.

"I know you miss your mom. But that's okay." She
wiped a tear from Lori's cheek. "My mother was in a
car accident, too. I still miss her."

Lori looked at her. "Really?"

"My dad was in that accident, too, but every day
I'm glad he's here. And now you have a daddy."

Lisa pursed her lips, then scratched her thumb. "I
want it to be different."

"I know, sweetheart, but sometimes things aren't the
way we want them. When I was sixteen, I was in a car
accident and broke both of my legs." Toni didn't mention that her date had been killed.

"Your dad told us about it," Lisa observed.

"And I didn't like sitting around while my friends
went to school. That's when my dad bought me my
first bird. His name was Sugar. I learned all about ca-
naries. Then I went on to study about other birds. I
found that I loved studying them. What you have to do
is find something that you like and enjoy the situation."

They both carefully studied Toni until Sam sat down
in the midst of them. Both girls reached out to him.

"I like Sam," Lisa offered.

Lori agreed with a nod.

Things weren't going well. If Toni wasn't careful,
Zach would have to get a dog in addition to all the
other changes in his life.

"What's that funny smell?" Lisa asked, wrinkling
her nose.

"The pancakes," Toni yelled, jumping to her feet.

Quickly she scooped up the burnt pancakes and threw them into the sink.

She glanced at the girls.

"Did you burn all of them?" Lisa asked, peeking into the sink.

"I have more batter. I'll make more."

"'Kay. But maybe you should watch them."

Toni wanted to laugh. Lisa was a pistol. When she looked at Lori, she appeared worried. The child needed to be reassured. "All right, let's try again and this time we'll all watch them."

"Yippee!"

They were almost finished with their breakfast when Zach showed up. He looked far too handsome for Toni's peace of mind. A strand of his thick hair fell onto his forehead, giving her the crazy desire to brush it back.

"How's your side?" Toni asked as they walked to the kitchen.

"A little sore, but that's to be expected." He stopped by the table. "Good morning," he greeted the girls.

"We're having pancakes," Lisa informed him. She placed the last bite on her plate into her mouth.

"They're good," Lori added.

"Would you like something to eat, Zach? Or maybe a cup of coffee?" Toni asked.

"Just coffee," he replied, sitting down at the table.

"Have you eaten?" Toni persisted.

"I can get something later."

"This batter will just go to waste if I don't cook it," Toni informed him as she gave him a cup of coffee.

He appeared reluctant, then nodded.

"Good." She turned on the grill again.

"But don't talk to her," Lisa piped in. "She might burn them."

Toni knew she was turning beet red.

The corner of his mouth twitched. "But you ate yours," Zach noted, looking at Lisa's empty plate.

"That's 'cause she cooked some more after she burned 'em."

"But she didn't burn those, did she?"

"She did okay, but the bad ones are in the sink." She wrinkled her nose. "Can't you smell 'em? They were icky."

Well, so much for her adventure into motherhood, Toni thought. The girls were warning their dad about her cooking.

"I'm willing to try," Zach reassured his daughter.

His confidence touched Toni's heart. When her eyes met his, he smiled and lifted his coffee cup to her.

"She makes good coffee," he added.

"Ick," Lisa replied. "I'm done. So's Lori. Can we go play with Sam?" She looked at Toni.

Toni nodded.

Lisa raced from the room, then stopped at the door to wait for her sister.

"Did ya know that Toni broke her legs just like Lori?" Lisa added.

Zach looked at Toni, who was pretending to concentrate on the pancakes on the grill. "Yes."

"Well," Lisa continued, "her daddy bought her a bird, so she wouldn't be lonely. Lisa and I like Sam. Could we keep him?"

Toni whipped her head around to face the others, her eyes wide. It appeared her worries about the dog were well-founded. Before she could answer, Zach spoke.

"Sam's a great dog, but he belongs to Toni's dad."

"We could ask him if he would give us Sam," Lisa logically offered.

"Toni's dad would miss him," Zach told her.

"Lisa, honey," Toni said before Zach said anything else. "I bought Sam for my dad when my mother died. We can ask him, but Sam helped him when he missed my mother. They are good friends. How would you feel if your best friend went away?"

Lisa pursed her lips, moving them from side to side. Finally, she nodded. "'Kay." She dashed out of the room. Lori followed.

Still stunned, Toni turned back to the grill and flipped the pancakes. She heard Zach's chair move, then felt his presence behind her. Wishing her nerve endings wouldn't dance every time the man was close to her, she glanced over her shoulder and tried to smile. "I'm sorry about that. The girls were missing their mother, and I tried to help, but things got confused."

Zach leaned back against the counter. "I'm glad to hear that it happens to someone else besides me. I've found myself in that situation several times over the past two days." He shook his head. "Damn, you'd think after leading a team of special commandos, that two four-year-old girls wouldn't be a problem."

"No, I wouldn't think that. Little girls are formidable for any male to deal with. Just ask my dad."

Zach laughed.

"But he survived having three daughters."

Zach nodded. After taking a big gulp of his coffee, he said, "I talked to the landlord in my complex. There's a two-bedroom furnished apartment available. I moved my things into it this morning."

"Oh." Her response popped out of her mouth before

she thought. "You certainly have been efficient." Toni placed the pancakes on a plate and handed it to him.

He stood studying her. "Is there a problem?"

She refilled her coffee cup, then sat at the table. He joined her.

"What's wrong, Toni?" His voice was soft and intimate, making her want things that couldn't be.

She shrugged. "As I told you before, I just think that apartments aren't the best place to raise children."

"I don't have a choice. I knew I was coming to get the girls, and we need a bigger place immediately."

"You're right."

She watched as he buttered and drowned his pancakes in syrup. Did he have any idea how to meet the complex needs of four-year-old girls?

"Since I know nothing about children, I wanted to ask you what I need to do for them."

Toni felt an odd sense of relief. He was serious about taking care of the girls. He'd asked for her help, and at least he didn't pretend that he knew what to do.

"The first thing I would do is see about enrolling the girls in a preschool. There are several close to the office that take four-year-olds. Are you planning to leave them there all day?"

"I hope to hire a housekeeper."

At least the man was making plans for his daughters. "In addition to a preschool, Lori is going to need to see a doctor about her leg. I have the name of a good orthopedist that I could give you. She's the partner of the doctor who took care of me when I broke my legs."

Leaning back in his chair, his gaze focused on her. "Your story about your accident seemed to impress the girls."

"I wanted them to know I understood how they felt."

"That was the accident where your date was killed, wasn't it?"

Toni gave him a surprised look.

He shrugged. "Your dad told me about the tanker broadsiding your date's car when you were going to your junior prom."

"Oh." She fell silent, then whispered, "I never got to dance a single dance at that prom or my senior one, since I couldn't walk well my senior year, either."

The words tumbled out of her mouth before she thought. With a blush staining her cheeks, she glanced at Zach. He stared down into his coffee mug.

After her initial embarrassment faded, she admitted that maybe the knowledge of her struggle would help him with Lori and some of the things the little girl would go through. "My legs were broken in several places. I spent a lot of time in bed. I had good days and bad. Sometimes I would dream about the accident and wake up screaming for Bobby Ray to be careful, but we were always hit."

She bit her bottom lip, not wanting to reveal all her demons, but she was sure that Zach would need the knowledge. "There were some days I felt guilty for surviving the accident and cried. And there were days when I was mad that I lived, and Bobby Ray died. I'm sure Lori will go through something like that. It will help her if she has someone she can talk to about her feelings."

"So, you're telling me that Lori might need counseling." His tone was quiet and thoughtful.

"Yes." She braced herself, thinking that he might ask her to take Lori to counseling for him.

Nodding, he said, "I'll check into seeing who is the most qualified to talk with Lori. Do you think Lisa will also need help?"

His question amazed her. That he would even think about Lisa gave her a warm feeling. "Good question. Lisa was in the car with her mother and Lori, so it couldn't hurt to check into it."

"All right."

She waited, expecting him to ask for more advice or shift his responsibility for the girls onto someone else.

"Thank you for your help."

When he stood, she blinked at him stupidly, amazed at his actions. He walked into the living room. "Girls, it's time to go."

The girls glanced at Toni, then their dad. They looked like two convicts going to their execution. As Zach opened the door, Lisa ran to Toni and hugged her leg, then hugged Sam's neck.

As they drove away, a tear ran down Toni's cheek, and in her heart there was a sad emptiness.

Zach had had easier days. Facing terrorists with M16s or bombs made with plastic explosives seemed like a cakewalk to him after spending the day with his four-year-old twin girls. Logic could be used with a terrorist. Passion, hatred, greed could also be used. Those were all emotions that he knew and could deal with. But what drove a little girl's mind? For that matter, what drove any female's mind?

Why aren't there any mountains? Who's going to take care of us? I have to tinkle. What's for dinner? I hate broccoli.

They lucked out with the doctor that Toni had suggested. She had a cancellation that afternoon and was able to see Lori. The doctor had been very reassuring to Zach, telling him that Lori should be out of the cast soon. She could discard the crutches.

But there his luck had ended. Signing them up for preschool had been a hellish experience. The woman who ran the center must have taken lessons from his old drill instructor. She cut him no slack.

"Hurry up, Daddy. I'm hungry," Lisa commented from the back seat. "'Sides, I want to see Toni again."

Zach glanced at Lori by his side. "Are you eager to see her, too."

Lori smiled shyly. "Yes. I hope Sam's there, too."

"Sure he will be," Lisa said with the confidence only a child could manage.

Zach wondered if he was gambling on a losing hand by hoping that Toni would be home. When the girls had asked for pizza for dinner again tonight, he'd relented, as their lives so suddenly had been turned upside down. When they asked if they could share the pizza with Toni, he welcomed the excuse to see her.

It's for the girls' sake, he reassured himself. But the words didn't ring true in his brain.

When he turned down her street and spotted her house, an odd feeling flashed through his brain. Home. No, that wasn't it. It had to be relief.

As soon as he stopped the car in the driveway of Toni's home, Lisa was out of the car, running up to the door.

"Toni, Toni, are you home?" She pounded on the door. A dog's bark greeted her words. Lisa squealed with delight. "Toni, this is Lisa. And Lori and our dad. Hurry up and answer the door."

Zach was helping Lori out of the car when the front

door opened. The woman who stood there was a little shorter than Toni, with blond hair and intense eyes.

"You're not Toni," Lisa clearly stated.

"That's right. I'm her sister, J.D." the woman offered.

"Oh." Lisa's disappointment rang in her voice.

"Hi, Lisa," Toni said as she stepped to her sister's side.

"You're here," Lisa cried. "We brought you some pizza and ice cream."

Toni stepped outside, and Sam followed her. He eagerly greeted Lisa. Toni's gaze settled on Zach as he helped Lori with her crutches.

"We didn't mean to barge in," he began, "but the girls and I wanted to share our dinner with you. If you have company—" He shrugged. "We should've called."

The look of disappointment on both girls' faces made Toni face him. "J.D. just stopped by for a visit. She's flying back to Dallas tonight, so I'll have to eat alone if you don't stay."

Both girls looked at their father with pleading eyes. Zach never knew what a sucker he was for those glances until he encountered the twins. "If you're sure we won't put you out..."

"You'll be doing me a favor. I didn't get to send Sam home, and he's been whining, wanting someone to play with." The dog took that moment to drop a tennis ball at Lisa's feet.

Against the tide, he didn't stand a chance. "All right."

"Yippee," cried Lisa. Lori grinned, an expression that Zach hadn't seen before this moment.

Zach gathered up the pizza box and the sack containing the ice cream and walked to the door. J.D. continued to hold the glass storm door open for him. He could hear Lisa and Lori talking to Toni in the living room.

"Did you have a busy day?" Toni asked the girls.

"Yeah. Lori saw a doctor about her leg, then we went to the place where we're going to play and learn our letters."

Zach walked into the kitchen and set the pizza on the table. When he opened the sack with the ice cream, he looked around for the refrigerator.

"I'll take that," J.D. offered, then put the container in the freezer. Turning, she studied Zach. "So, you're the head of security for my dad's firm."

Zach felt like a felon, being grilled. Her voice had that lawyer quality, stern and no-nonsense. "Yes, that's what I do for your dad."

"I've heard a lot about you," J.D. said. "Even seen you a couple of times when I've been here in Midland. When Toni told me about your problem, I'll admit I was surprised."

Zach had a feeling that J.D. wasn't simply making small talk. "Your sister has been a big help."

"Did my father ever mention that I'm married to a detective with the Dallas PD? My sister in Saddle is married to a deputy sheriff. And we have a half brother who's a Texas Ranger."

Zach heard the warning in her voice. She was showing her hand and letting him know she had firepower in her corner.

"Yes, he's mentioned it several times. In fact, your dad introduced me to Rafe when he came here the first time."

J.D. studied him for several moments, then nodded.

"Good. I just wanted you to be aware of all the members of this family."

"And why is that?"

"Protection, Mr. Knight, for you." *And Toni.* She didn't say it, but he read the warning in her eyes.

"What's going on in here?" Toni asked from the doorway, taking in both her sister and Zach.

J.D. smiled. "Zach and I were just trading goodbyes." She leaned over and kissed Toni on the cheek. "Take care of yourself, and don't let Dad get away with anything." She grabbed her purse and walked out to the car parked in front of the house.

Toni turned to Zach. "What were you really talking about?"

Chapter 5

"We were discussing your family," Zach casually replied, not meeting her eyes.

Toni had had a bad feeling when she walked into the kitchen earlier and saw her sister with Zach. There'd been a militant look in J.D.'s eyes, the same kind of look she showed when she was in the courtroom, cross-examining an opposing witness.

"What about my family?" Toni replied.

The corner of Zach's mouth pulled up. "She was telling me about all the law officers there were. I knew about the Ranger, but not the others."

Although her oldest sister would never admit it, J.D. was a chip off the old block. She was fiercely protective of her youngest sister, as was their father. "I'm sorry about that. It's a family trait. It's a toss-up between J.D. and Dad as to who has the hardest head."

Zach's gaze captured hers. In the depths of his green

eyes a warmth and understanding burned. "Don't apologize. It's a gift."

His words surprised her. She wanted to investigate his remark, but from the closed look on his face, she knew he wouldn't offer anything more.

"I'm hungry," Lisa chimed from the doorway. "So's Lori."

Toni looked over her shoulder at the twins standing in the doorway. "I'll get the plates," Toni told the girls, "and your dad will dish out the pizza."

"We didn't get all those yucky things on it this time. Only pepp—" She scrunched her nose.

"Pepperoni," Zach supplied.

Lisa nodded. "That's it. The round thingies." She looked pleased with herself.

Toni's amused gaze met Zach's. They shared the small humor of the moment. The intimacy of it hit Toni hard. She turned and regathered her composure as she pulled out paper plates and napkins from the cabinet.

The girls happily bit into their pizza.

"How did the day go?" Toni asked.

"It was 'kay," Lisa replied casually before anyone could respond. Toni bit back a smile at the remark. It was quickly becoming clear that Lisa's favorite word was *'kay*. And she was also becoming the family spokesman, whether Zach liked it or not.

"What did y'all do?" She looked at the girls, then Zach.

"We went to the doctor for Lori," Lisa continued.

"Dad said that you went to that doctor, too," Lori remarked, "but you went to the old guy."

Toni was sure that Dr. Richards would laugh at Lori's assessment of him. It was accurate but not flattering. "Yes, I went to Dr. Richards. Dr. Conroy, who you saw, just came to Midland last year. I hear she is very nice. And that you got good news.''

Lori nodded.

"Then we saw our new school," Lisa added. "Dad didn't like Mrs. Shaw.''

The giggle Toni tried to swallow sounded like a snort. She felt the others stare at her. Finally, Toni stole a glance at Zach. Nothing showed on his face as he continued to eat his pizza.

"Oh? Why do you say that?" Toni asked.

Lisa took a bite of her pizza. "Dad had a frown on his face when he was talking to her.'' She paused and took a drink. "I'm glad he doesn't look at us like that anymore.''

The girls went back to their pizza. Zach's gaze met hers. His was stoic and remote, but Toni sensed there was a hurt buried deep inside.

"Do you like your new apartment?" Toni asked, hoping to smooth over the awkward spot.

"It's got bedrooms," Lisa replied. "One for Dad and one for me and Lori. We don't have a yard, like you have here. And there's no swings.''

"But you have your very own bed.''

"Yeah, but there are no toys there. And no dog.'' Disappointment rang in her voice.

Toni noted that Lori's face echoed her sister's disappointment as she stared down at her plate.

"Your daddy wasn't expecting you. You need to give him some time to understand about girls. He's a boy and boys don't think like girls.''

"Yeah, they like bugs and lizards and dirt.''

Toni avoided looking at Zach for fear she would burst out laughing. "That's true. But when they get older, they like—" Football, cars and guns. "When you get older, you'll understand about boys. You'll like them.''

Neither girl appeared convinced by her arguments. Lisa folded her arms over her chest. ''I don't think I will.''

After they finished a bowl of ice cream, the girls settled in front of the TV and watched a video. Sam joined them.

As Toni and Zach cleaned up the kitchen, Toni studied him.

''So, how did your day really go?''

''Lisa wasn't far off the mark. Lori should be off her crutches by next week.''

''And what about the director of the preschool?'' Toni inquired.

''Lisa didn't miss that one, either. The woman reminded me of an old drill instructor I had. Took no excuses, cut no one any slack. But she seemed to be able to talk to the girls. Maybe it was just me the woman objected to.''

''That's a good description of Marge's attitude.'' Toni loaded the glasses and utensils into the dishwasher. ''She's a wonderful administrator, a friend of my sister's, but she doesn't do warm, fuzzy with the parents.''

''Ah, that explains it.'' Zach threw the last of the napkins into the trash. ''I watched the girls with the other teachers. They did a good job with both Lisa and Lori.''

''Sounds like you're all set.''

Zach leaned back against the counter and folded his arms over his chest. ''I have another question I want to ask you.''

''Sure. What is it?''

"The girls didn't come with too many things in their suitcases. I know they need some underthings and clothes, but I don't have any idea what. Do you have some suggestions?"

Toni remembered the things the girls had in their bags when she put them to bed the first night. "I see. What we need to do is make a little trip to the department store."

"I didn't mean that you should put yourself out."

Toni couldn't prevent the big grin that bubbled up. "You are many things, Zachary Knight, but I really don't see you whizzing through the children's section buying panties. But you could buy Lori plain ones, and I'll bet Lisa would love the panties that are embroidered with the days of the week, and maybe that would help tell the difference between Lori's and Lisa's."

A look of amazement crossed Zach's normally stoic face. "Panties with the days on them?"

"Written across the seat."

His eyes were still wide. "Amazing."

"Zach, I don't ever get to go shopping for little girl things, except when I buy gifts for my sisters' girls. This could be fun."

She started out of the kitchen, then stopped abruptly and turned, running into Zach's chest. His arms closed around her, keeping her from falling. The strength of him under her hands was heady, making her heart pump wildly.

It reminded her of the time last year when he brought her home from the company Christmas party after he had rescued her from Carl. Zach had driven her home and escorted her to the front door. When she had lifted her lips to his, he'd backed away and said good-night.

Humiliation and shock had raced through her. Obviously, she'd been the only one to feel the attraction. After smarting for several days, Toni had decided Zach was too much like her father for her to even think about giving in to the feelings he stirred.

But right now, being held in his arms, Toni could see that Zach felt the electricity that arced between them as clearly as she did. It was not a comforting thought.

She felt Zach's hands on her back, then his arms fell away.

"If you don't want me to accompany you, it won't be a problem. I could make a list of the things you could get."

Zach threw his head back. "A smart man realizes when he's out of his element." He shook his head. "That was one of the problems my ex-wife had with me. Except for making love, she said I knew nothing about women."

Toni nearly swallowed her tongue with his last admission, and the repercussions of his words rang through her mind. *Except for making love...*

"I need help here. Anything you could tell me or show me would be appreciated."

"I'll admit there aren't too many terrorists at the department store—except maybe a few grade school boys who are driving their mothers crazy."

Zach grinned. His expression was so unexpected and charming, that it went straight to her heart. She was sinking so fast she could barely catch her breath. How could any woman be seduced by a couple of four-year-olds and a very masculine smile? She needed her head examined.

Taking a deep breath, she heard herself say, "Let's go tell the girls we're going shopping."

* * *

Relief washed over Zach in waves as Toni picked up another package of socks for the girls. Shopping for girls was worse than running the obstacle course in the rain. Damn, who knew so much stuff existed? Pink-and-purple underthings. And little flowers all over everything. Lisa wanted flowers; Lori liked plain colors.

"Zach, do you have bedding for that new bed you have in your apartment?" Toni asked.

He stared at her. "I have a set of sheets."

"A set—as in one?" Toni asked, amazement coloring her eyes.

"Why would I need more than that?"

Toni leaned down and whispered to the girls, "Sometimes boys don't get better."

They giggled and Zach knew he was outgunned.

"Do you have detergent to wash all these new things we're buying?"

He shook his head. "I just usually take my laundry to the cleaners. They do it. There's nothing to worry about."

Toni looked at him as if he were a lost pup. "You must feel like you've stepped into another world," she added, softly.

She didn't know the half of it. But Zach wasn't going to let a little ignorance defeat him. The girls were his and he'd take care of them, no matter what. "I have. But that doesn't mean I can't learn. I didn't know about being a soldier until I went to boot camp. I guess I can consider this my training."

"All right. I'll give you a crash course in laundry products and cleaning supplies."

"Is there anything else?" He felt like a man trying

to stop the *Titanic* from sinking. He was bailing and bailing and still going down.

"Lots, but I think we might start off slow."

Zach could only thank heaven.

Of all the scenes that had played themselves out in her mind, never had Toni imagined the one that occurred that night with Zach. They had taken the items that they had purchased at the store and come back to Toni's house. It was there Toni showed Zach the intricacies of doing laundry. Much to his credit, Zach knew some of the basics, but he looked relieved when she showed him how to do the girls' clothing.

Again, the girls bedded down in Toni's spare room, with Sam sleeping between them.

"I think Sam and the girls have formed an attachment," Toni said as she poured two more cups of coffee.

"Yeah, I think so, but Sam belongs to your dad, and the girls have to realize that he's not theirs."

"Maybe you could get them a pet of their own. The shelters are full of dogs and cats that need a home."

Zach considered her suggestion. "I'll think about it. Right now, I'm trying to keep from drowning. I don't know if a pet might sink my ship."

He had a point.

As they waited for the dryer to finish the last load of laundry, Zach asked, "Do you have any pointers on bath time and other things?"

His question brought a warm feeling. Zach might not know diddly about little girls, but at least he was trying to learn. "Until Lori gets her cast off, she won't be able to get it wet. You'll have to wrap the cast in a plastic garbage bag and tape it so the cast stays dry, then let her hang her leg over the side of the tub.''

From his expression, she would've guessed that she'd just asked him to jump off a cliff.

''Lisa will probably be easier to deal with. You can wash her hair as often as it needs to be done. I'd ask them how often their mother did it for them. It will give you a clue as to how frequently you'll need to do it.''

He stared at his cup. Although he had not voiced a single complaint since she'd found him and the girls days ago, there was a desolation in his eyes that tugged at her heart.

Her hand lightly rested on his. The electricity that was always there between them erupted like a lightning storm. When the girls were awake, they were a good buffer between them. But here in her kitchen, late at night with only the two of them, the need that lurked under the surface surged. Her eyes met his and Toni felt the heat shoot through her body.

His hand covered hers and his thumb gently caressed her knuckles. With each stroke, the tension in her stomach increased. Suddenly it was hard to draw breath into her lungs. His gaze dropped to her lips. She felt his look as strongly as if he touched her.

His head lowered, his eyes never wavering from hers. She understood that he was giving her time to back away from the kiss. But much to her surprise her heart didn't want to back away. She remembered all the reasons why she shouldn't be attracted to Zach, but the vibrant pull of his eyes silenced all those voices.

His lips brushed lightly over hers, like the whisper of the wind through the trees. He seemed to gauge her reaction. When he read her desire, her welcome, his lips settled gently on hers. Softly, with infinite care, he coaxed her mouth to follow his.

His fingers came up to rest on the pulse point beneath her ear and his thumb smoothed over her neck.

A thousand impulses swamped Toni's brain. The taste of him, his heat, the rough feel of the pads of his fingers. Toni's hand came up to rest on his forearm. His muscles were like steel covered with warm skin.

She was falling deeper and deeper into the feelings that he evoked until she heard ringing.

Zach pulled back and looked down at her. "The dryer is done."

His words made no sense. She stupidly looked at him. "Dryer?" What kind of romantic thing was that to say?

"The sheets in the dryer are done."

The ding sounded again, reminding Toni where they were and why they were sitting in the kitchen. She nodded, feeling like a fool. "The sheets." She jumped to her feet and walked into the utility room. Taking several deep breaths to calm her racing heart, Toni scolded herself. Obviously, Zach hadn't been as overwhelmed by their kiss as she had. Her hands rested on her burning cheeks. Darn.

She retrieved the sheets from the dryer and brought them into the kitchen and set them on the table.

Zach stood and picked up several socks and panties that had fallen out from the clothes.

"Since you probably haven't had to fold anything like this, I'll show you how I do it, then you'll be on your own."

He nodded.

Zach watched her silently. She wanted to say something about the kiss, but what? If she was honest with herself, kissing Zach was something she'd wanted to do for a long time. Her nerves were always on full alert every time he was near, but Zach hid his reaction behind those steely green eyes of his. Tonight she'd caught a glimpse of something else…desire, need, hunger. Toni wasn't sure what he felt, but she did know he'd reacted.

After she'd placed all the clean, folded clothes into a laundry basket, she dared to look at him. His cool mask of control was back in place.

"Well, how did you like your first foray into doing laundry?" she asked, trying for lightness.

"I think I'll hire a housekeeper," he honestly admitted.

"It's less daunting the second time through."

"I'll take your word for it." He grabbed the laundry basket and headed toward his car. Toni replaced the detergent into the sack and carried it out to his new car. Gone was the little 280ZX and in its place was a Jeep. She handed him the sack.

"If you don't want to wake the girls, they are more than welcome to spend the night again."

Zach glanced at his watch. It was close to eleven-thirty. "Do you mind?"

"They were wiped out after we came back from the store. I don't mind them staying here. But I'll warn you, I have a nine o'clock class to teach."

He nodded. "Then I'll be here by eight."

She smiled at him, wanting to erase their kiss. Unsure how he felt, she didn't want to reveal her heart to him.

"Thanks for the basic training in parenthood." That devastating smile of his, the one that sent her heart into overdrive, curved his lips.

"I'm glad I could help."

As she watched him drive away, Toni's feelings were whirling with the force of a tornado. And what it was leaving behind was destruction.

Zach put the new sheets on the girls' bed and tried to put away the clothes they'd bought. Suddenly he was Mr. Mom and stupid. And not just in the fatherhood department. What had he been thinking when he'd kissed Toni?

She'd helped so much, he'd let his guard down and given in to the feelings that she always seemed to arouse in him. Not only did he have to fight the attraction that he felt for her now—had felt for her since the first time he'd laid eyes on her. But he also had to fight his desire for that female touch in his life to deal with the girls.

He was in twice the trouble he had been a week ago, before the children entered his life.

Damn. How had things gotten so out of control?

Well, it wasn't the girls' fault that his ex had hated his guts. Nor was it their fault she'd been killed. And although Zach had walked blind into this situation, he had to deal with it. But what he could control in the future was not kissing Toni Anderson again.

Just remembering the taste of her lips and the look in her eyes, made him ache and want more.

He couldn't go that direction again. Sylvia had cured him of the marriage fantasy. And even if she hadn't, his mother had been no sterling example. He'd been the product of an affair between a married man and his mom. After the affair ended, neither parent had much use for him, and Zach had grown up unloved and unsupervised.

He stopped his mind from reliving those ugly memories. Tomorrow, before he picked up the girls, Zach would find the name of a service that hired housekeepers. That would take care of laundry, housecleaning and meals.

As he stretched out on his bed, he remembered the taste of Toni's lips and wondered if the skin under her ear would taste as sweet.

Damn, he was in trouble.

Chapter 6

Toni glanced down at the banana pudding on the car seat next to her. She wondered if the girls and Zach would like it.

The driver behind her honked his horn, bringing her back from her mental wandering to the street where she needed to pay attention to the traffic. She started to drive.

It had been nearly a week and a half since she'd heard from Zach, and her curiosity had gotten the better of her. She'd made homemade banana pudding and decided that the twins needed a treat.

Pulling into the parking lot of the apartment building, she parked, grabbed the dish of pudding, her purse, and headed to Zach's apartment.

When she rang the doorbell, she heard a muffled shout, followed by a loud thud and then the sound of a smoke detector.

The door opened a crack and Lisa looked up at Toni.

"Hi," she greeted Toni. "Daddy, it's Toni," she shouted over the noise. The alarm stopped, leaving the scene deathly quiet. "And she's carrying somethin'. Hurry and open the door."

Zach appeared a moment later at the door and unlatched the chain. "Hello." He looked like a man wrestling an alligator and losing.

A self-conscious smile curved Toni's mouth. "I didn't mean to disturb you, but I made some banana pudding and thought y'all would enjoy it."

"Can you come inside and cook?" Lisa asked Toni. Lori appeared by her sister's side. "Daddy just burned the meal the lady left." The child waved her arms to fan away the smoke.

Toni gave Lori a puzzled frown. "What lady?"

"The housekeeper," Zach supplied.

"Yeah, and she quit today," Lisa added innocently. "I don't know why."

Toni got the distinct impression that Lisa knew exactly why the woman had quit.

A dull flush colored Zach's face.

"I'd be happy to help any way I could," Toni offered.

Zach hesitated a moment, then said, "I'd appreciate it." He stepped away from the door and motioned Toni inside. "Things got out of hand."

From the awful smell and drifting smoke, she could well imagine.

They went immediately to the kitchen. Sitting in the sink was a skillet filled with spaghetti sauce burned to the bottom of the pan.

"I guess I turned the burner on too high, then forgot about it," Zach admitted.

"It happens to all of us. If you have some ground

beef and tomato sauce, we could make more sauce for the spaghetti.''

''We?'' Zach replied.

''That's a figure of speech. Do you have more meat?''

''In the refrigerator. And there's tomato sauce in the cupboard.''

''Then we can save dinner,'' Toni replied.

''Yeah!'' chimed the girls.

''Aside from tonight's cooking mishap, how have things been going?'' Toni asked Zach as they cleaned up the kitchen. She had volunteered to load the dishwasher and clean up the pans, while Zach dried them and put them away.

He shrugged. ''I've been on easier missions.''

Toni's startled gaze found his.

''I've done easier things,'' he amended his statement. ''It seems the girls have a certain talent for running off housekeepers. I don't know if it's on purpose, or just the result of having two little girls.'' Zach shook his head.

''Well, all children have times of—''

He rested his hip on the counter next to her. Toni felt his warmth as if she stood close to a fireplace during a bad winter storm.

''Yes?'' He waited expectantly for her to finish.

''Acting up. Maybe the girls are worried that you, too, will leave them, and are trying you to see how you'll respond.''

He rubbed his chin as he thought about that. Toni had the crazy urge to touch his face, run her fingers over his lips and— She stopped her wayward thoughts, and concentrated on the skillet in the sink.

"That could explain their actions with the house-keepers. Both women were efficient and good cooks."

"Zach, what the girls are looking for is an emotional connection. Their behavior is not that unusual. Have you taken them to a counselor or psychologist?"

He shook his head.

"Talking about their fears might help. It also might help you."

From his expression, Toni knew she had just stepped on his toes. She rinsed off the pan and placed it in the drainer.

He picked it up and slowly dried it.

"Other than running off the housekeepers, is there any other question I could answer for you?" she asked.

"Is asking for fourteen glasses of water after they've gone to bed natural?" He sounded completely bewildered.

Laughter bubbled up. She leaned against the sink and smiled at him. "When I was young, my dad used to keep a nightly tally of how many times I needed water and bathroom breaks. I think he announced the record was ten in one hour. I held the record among my sisters."

A slow, sexy smile curved his mouth. "I can identify with his frustration."

"It's common. And I think as time goes on, Zach, that the girls will settle down. Has there been anything else?" She dried her hands.

"They tried to run the scam on me of switching identities, only it backfired on them. Since Lori has her cast on, I nailed them the first time they tried it. I guess they were so used to doing it, it didn't occur to them the cast told them apart."

"Good job." Toni glanced down at her watch. "It's late and I should go."

She took a step and ended up inches from him. Toni had to stop herself from reaching out and running her fingers over Zach's strong chin. She'd been attracted to him from the first moment she saw him, but watching him struggle to be a father to the girls went straight to her heart, multiplying her desire.

His hand came up and tucked a stray lock of hair behind her ear. "Thanks for your help." His head started to lower, then he stopped himself and took a step away from her.

After saying goodbye to the girls, Toni paused at the front door.

"Try another housekeeper, Zach. Eventually, the girls will realize that they can't run everyone off."

"I'll do it. And Toni—" He paused, then whispered, "Good night."

As she drove home, Toni wondered what Zach had wanted to say. She wished she could as easily turn off the feelings that Zachary Knight ignited in her.

"I quit."

Zach stared at the elderly woman as she picked up her purse. He'd come home a little later than his normal time, expecting things to be under control at the apartment. No such luck.

"You can mail me my wages." She strode to the door and looked back at the girls. "Good luck. I hope you survive." With a militant look, she slammed the door behind her.

Zach's gaze moved from the closed door to his twins, sitting on the couch. Lori bit her lip, and Lisa smiled innocently at him. This housekeeper-sitter lasted two days before she'd quit. It appeared his girls were good at running off help.

Zach slipped off his sport coat and hung it over the back of a chair. "Do you have any idea why Mrs. O'Neal left?" Zach calmly asked. He realized early on that if he was going to get any information out of the girls, he had to use a calm and quiet voice, no matter if he felt like shouting.

"Nope," Lisa gaily answered. Her answer was just a little too pat to relieve Zach.

Zach looked at Lori. "Do you have any idea why Mrs. O'Neal quit?"

"I don't know," she quietly answered and looked to her sister for support. "Maybe it was—"

Lisa popped up and ran over to where the fishbowl sat on the low bookcase and frowned. "Daddy, are the fishies suppose' to be floating upside down?"

He strode across the room and one glance at the bowl told Zach that the goldfish were dead. Next to the bowl was an empty container of fish food. Looking at the bottom of the bowl, Zach discovered a large amount of food.

"No, fish don't swim upside down. They're dead."

"How come?" Lisa asked. "They weren't in an accident like Mom."

Lisa's innocent words brought Zach up short. The girls had gone through so much in the past month and they didn't need him to lose it by shouting at them.

"No," he answered.

Lisa looked up at him. "Can we bury 'em?"

From the expression in her eyes and Lori's, Zach knew he didn't have a choice.

"Sure."

After the miniburial under the bushes beside the

apartments, they ate the dinner Mrs. O'Neal had left. It was a couple of hours later after putting the girls to bed that Zach was able to sit down and go through the mail.

There were a couple of bills and a circular. But it was the last envelope in the stack, from Jones, Travis and Associates, Ltd., Attorneys at Law, that captured his attention.

Zach opened the letter and scanned the page. "Mr. Knight, We have been retained by Melanie Stafford to obtain appropriate order granting Ms. Stafford custody of her nieces, Lisa and Lori."

His eyes scanned the rest of the letter.

"...you will be notified directly of the preliminary hearing date. Sincerely, Michael Jones."

As Zach read the words, his anger built. He cursed, using several graphic phrases he'd learned in the military. He felt like smashing his fist into the wall, but he knew that would upset and frighten the girls.

Standing, he walked to the living room window. Looking out at the horizon, he wondered what the hell Melanie thought she was doing.

Getting back at you, his conscience whispered. Melanie had hated Zach from the first moment he went home with Sylvia. Melanie's feelings only increased in intensity after the divorce.

Taking a deep breath, he moved back to the table and reread the letter. What was he going to do? It didn't take him long to decide he'd get himself an attorney and fight for his daughters. He might not have known the girls existed until recently, but now that he knew, there was no way in hell he was going to give them up. He refused to do to his children what had been done to him.

He'd find a way to keep them, no matter the cost.

* * *

When Toni turned around from the blackboard where she had written her next point of the lecture, her eyes scanned the students. By the door stood Zachary Knight. He was an imposing figure of a man with the body that would be the envy of most men and the delight of any woman. His brown hair looked as if he'd run his hands through it countless times. When his penetrating eyes met hers, he nodded and took the closest available seat.

A million thoughts crowded her brain. Why was he here? Had something happened to the girls? Or maybe something had happened to her dad or the company.

Panic must have shown in her eyes because he shook his head slightly. Apparently, whatever brought him here, it wasn't crucial. He nodded for her to continue.

She finished her point, then answered several questions from her students. Glancing at the clock, she dismissed the class.

As she packed up her notes, she asked, "What are you doing here, Zach?"

"I need to talk to you, Toni." That sounded ominous.

Her head snapped up. "Why? Is something wrong?"

"There's a problem." He glanced around the room. "Could we go to your office?"

She swallowed, anxiety knotting her stomach. "Sure."

As they walked down the hall, Toni wondered what could've brought him here to the university. She hadn't seen him since the night she'd brought the banana pudding. Countless nights, she'd relived their time together. And she remembered the time before when he'd kissed her. The touch of his hands, the taste of his lips, the desire that overwhelmed her.

As they approached her office door, Beth, the department secretary, nodded at Zach. "I see you found Dr. Anderson." Her smile was flirtatious and Toni had the crazy urge to tell the secretary to grow up.

"Thank you for your help," he replied.

Once in her office, Toni set down her papers and settled in her chair. "Now, what is it that brought you here?"

He didn't sit down but walked to the window of her office and looked out.

"Is everything all right with the girls?" Toni blurted out, worried and nervous at his reticence.

He looked over his shoulder. "The girls are in fine form. They ran off another housekeeper." Facing her, he shook his head. "Whoever would've thought little girls had so much—"

"Devilry?"

From his expression, her description surprised him. "I'd call it talent."

"And have you compared notes with my dad yet? Remember, he had three girls."

The corner of his mouth kicked up. "It boggles the mind. He had some interesting stories. Did he ever have to bury your dead fish in the backyard?"

"Nope. But I did make Dad bury my pet lizard when it died."

"I don't even want to think about it." He shook his head. "But I didn't come here to talk about the girls' misadventures. I came here to propose to you."

"Propose what?"

"Marriage."

Toni felt her jaw drop. "I beg your pardon?"

"I want us to get married."

As a proposal, it lacked a certain charm.

"And why would you want to do that?" She was dying to hear his reasons.

"Because I need a wife."

Didn't all men, but she didn't voice her opinion. "Would you like to explain that statement to me?"

He sat down across from Toni. "Yesterday I received notification from my ex-sister-in-law that she is going to fight me for custody of the girls. I talked to one of the company lawyers this morning. And although he doesn't do family law, he told me I'd be in better shape with the courts if I was married."

Toni's heart thundered. She had had fantasies about Zach, of him sweeping her up in his arms and… But this cold-blooded approach to marriage definitely wasn't part of the fantasy. "Why ask me?"

"Because you and the girls seem to like each other."

She wasn't much impressed with his reasoning.

"And I know your dad's been trying to set you up with various men, wanting you to get married." He shrugged. "I thought this might be beneficial for you, too. It would solve several problems in one fell swoop."

Suddenly anger shot through her. "What makes you think that?" she demanded. She sounded defensive even to her own ears.

"Because I've heard him grumble about you being too picky."

Embarrassment rolled over Toni in waves. She didn't doubt for one instant that her father had said such a thing, or that everyone at Anderson knew of her father's desire to see her married. He tended to be very blind in certain areas. She remembered several times when people had stared at her, then shook their heads.

"I can deal with my dad," she tersely replied. "Why don't you just find a nice girl, court her and marry her?" Toni asked. "That would solve your problems."

"Because I don't want a real marriage." The harsh tone of the words reflected his feelings. "Love is a crock. What the world revolves around is lust. That is understandable. I just want the appearance of a marriage to keep my girls with me."

"I see." Zach certainly did have a dismal view of life and marriage.

"My first marriage was a disaster. Sylvia and I fell into lust, then married. It was a terrible mistake. We made each other miserable for a long time. The sex wasn't worth it. I vowed never to do it again."

"But you're asking me to marry you," Toni stated.

"Ours would be a business arrangement only. I wouldn't expect this to be a normal marriage."

That caught her attention. "What exactly do you mean?"

"Strictly platonic. No sex would be required."

"No sex," she repeated, unsure she'd heard right.

"That wouldn't be part of the bargain. We would be getting married to protect each other from outside influences—you from your dad messing in your life, me from the courts taking away my girls."

Well, he certainly did have a plan. And Toni didn't know what to say.

"I see I've surprised you." His voice had softened and his expression was less defensive.

She took a deep breath, gathering her scattered wits. "Yes, it's quite a surprise."

"If you're worried about your inheritance, I'll be happy to sign a prenuptial agreement."

Not once had she worried about her inheritance.

He stood. "Why don't you think about it, then get back to me in a day or two."

"All right. I'll consider it." Toni couldn't believe her ears that those words had come out of her mouth.

He moved to the door. "No matter what you decide, Toni, thanks for all your help with the girls." He smiled that killer smile of his that made her heart skip a beat, then left her staring at the empty door.

After several minutes, Beth appeared in her doorway. "Where's that incredible man I saw you with earlier?" she asked. The leer in Beth's eyes irritated Toni.

"He's gone."

Beth shook her head. "You've been holding out on us, haven't you, Toni? Where did you find him?"

"Zach works for my dad."

"Is he single?" Beth asked, eagerness in her voice. Here was someone willing to date Zach.

"Yes."

"Well, honey, you give him my name and number and tell him I'm ready, willing and able."

"He has twin four-year-old daughters who tend to be a handful," Toni warned.

Pursing her lips, Beth said, "Forget it. I don't need that kind of grief." With that final thought, she left.

Even though Beth was attracted to Zach, Toni realized that the twins would complicate Zach's marriage quest. And what would their treatment be like at the hands of a woman who married Zach in spite of the girls?

That thought weighed heavily upon Toni.

Toni stood and walked to the window. Zach's re-

quest had blown her away. She had expected him to
ask for help over the past few weeks, but not once had
he called her with a problem, even with all the domes-
tic help the girls had run off. She had to admire him
for his persistence.

Now, he was asking her to marry him so he could
keep his daughters. Although what Zach had proposed
was strictly a business arrangement, his actions touched
her heart. He wanted his children. That spoke volumes
for the man.

Another longing rose up in her. Being with the girls
had made Toni face a truth she had tried to bury. She
wanted children. She'd all but given up the dream of
having children, but now Zach was giving her the op-
portunity to be a mother to two little girls.

And if that wasn't enough, Zach was a handsome
man. It was a dream come true, except Zach was too
much like her father, a hard-driving man. And that trait
was one of the things that had kept Toni from giving
in to her feelings for Zach last year.

There were a million reasons why she should just
tell Zach to forget it. She remembered her disastrous
engagement. Unlike her father, who had gone through
a couple of wives, Mark was supposedly a sensitive
man, who was always mindful of her feelings. But in
the end, Mark had the same flaw her father possessed.
He'd been unfaithful, too. That day Toni discovered
Mark in bed with her best friend, Toni decided that
there wasn't a man on earth worth the grief they
caused. She hadn't looked for an involvement since
then.

But the bitterness of that afternoon seemed unim-
portant, compared to her thoughts about the girls. She
remembered them asleep in her spare bedroom and

later playing with Sam. Their giggles and endless questions.

And Zach's sexy smile.

She gathered up her purse and went home to a cold meal of leftover chicken and potatoes.

Finally, after hours of stewing over it, arguing with herself, Toni knew she couldn't walk away from them.

Just as the late evening news started, Toni called Zach at his apartment.

"Hello." His voice sparked a reaction in her.

"Zach, this is Toni. I've decided to take you up on your offer."

The long silence on the other end of the line made her nervous.

"Are you sure?"

"What, are you trying to talk me out of it?" She tried to make it a joke, but failed.

"I just want you to be sure about your decision."

"I'm sure."

"When could we fly to Las Vegas and get married?" he asked.

"You mean right away?"

"I wouldn't ask it, Toni, but I don't want to give the court any reason to take my girls."

She reviewed her schedule. "I have a class tomorrow, but Friday I'm free."

"All right, then why don't I make arrangements for us to fly to Vegas? Also, we need to see a lawyer tomorrow to have him or her draw up the prenup. Do you have one you prefer?"

"My sister has a friend in Odessa next to the university, and I think she could do the job."

"I'll let you take care of that."

Things were moving at light-speed. "I'll call you

tomorrow and let you know when to show up to sign
the agreement.''

''You've got it.''

''Then I'll talk to you tomorrow.''

When she hung up the receiver, she wondered if
she'd made a mistake.

Toni squirmed in her chair and looked around the
lawyer's office. She'd called Anna Nunez, a friend of
her sister's, last night and arranged to have a prenuptial
agreement drawn up. Anna agreed to do it and have it
ready for her and Zach to sign at three this afternoon.

Glancing at her watch, she noted it was already three
fifteen. Zach was late. This wasn't a good sign. Toni
glanced at the secretary and smiled tightly at her.

Where was he? Had he decided at the last minute to
back out?

Suddenly the door opened and Zach strode in. En-
ergy and power seemed to swirl around him.

''Sorry to be late. There was a problem that popped
up at work.''

Toni nodded to the secretary and they were shown
into Anna's office.

After the introductions, Anna looked at the couple.
''I've drawn up the papers that Toni asked for. It says
that you, Zachary Knight, will lay no claim on any
inheritance that Toni has from her father if you should
ever divorce.'' She continued to outline the simple document.

If Toni expected Zach to object, she was disappointed, which only emphasized the fact that all Zach
wanted was protection to keep his daughters. Any hidden fantasy Toni had about Zach using the girls to
marry her evaporated.

Zach took the document from Anna's hands and read it quickly, then boldly signed his name to it.

So much for love.

When they finished signing the papers, Anna leaned back in her chair. "If you need further help, I'll be happy to work with you."

"Thanks, Anna, for your fast work," Toni said.

As they were walking out of the office, Anna whispered in Toni's ear, "I can see why you were in a rush."

A blush rose in Toni's cheeks.

Once in the hall, Zach turned to Toni. "I've booked us on the two-fifty flight into Dallas tomorrow, where we catch our flight to Vegas. Is that all right with you?"

"Yes. I'll meet you at the airport about two-fifteen."

"Why don't the girls and I pick you up around two?"

Her eyes widened. "You intend to bring the girls?"

"When I told them this morning that we were getting married, I had two very happy children. They told me they wanted to come, and forgave me for refusing to replace the dead goldfish. I couldn't say no."

Toni's eyes misted. His attitude toward the children was like rain after a long drought. His thoughtfulness was unexpected, welcomed.

But above all, it was dangerous.

Toni sat in her kitchen, picked up one of the chocolate chip cookies she'd just baked and took a bite. She glanced at the clock on the wall. Two-thirty in the morning. She'd tried for hours to sleep, but had given up and walked into the kitchen to bake her favorite comfort food.

This was the night before her marriage. Instead of her head being filled with the thoughts of being a new bride and being surrounded by family and friends, Toni was alone, questioning her sanity. And since she'd taken Sam back to her dad's, she didn't even have a dog to keep her company.

Why was she really marrying Zach? Was it strictly to be a mother to his daughters? Or was there another motive buried in her heart?

Zach certainly couldn't be accused of trying to pull the wool over her eyes with his proposal. He needed a wife and had asked her. Period. End of the story.

Too bad she wanted it to be more.

If things were going to work, then she needed to concentrate on the girls. She would try to do that and prayed she could pull it off.

As Zach got the girls dressed for their trip to the airport, he wondered if he was doing the right thing. He wanted to keep the girls, but was it right to use Toni? Had there been another way?

Although he hadn't hidden his agenda from Toni, he had to admit his proposal had been cold-blooded. But then again, his ex-wife had told him more than once that he didn't have a heart.

"Daddy, can I take my panties with the days on them?" Lisa asked. They were his daughter's pride and joy and she had to have on the right one each morning.

"Sure."

Lisa smiled and scampered back into her bedroom. He walked in behind her and checked the suitcase that contained the girls' things. Lori sat on the bed, hugging her new stuffed animal. He sat beside her.

"Are you excited about our trip?" he asked. Of the

two girls, Lori was the one who concerned him the most. He wondered if she was always this quiet, or had the accident made her more reserved?

When she looked up, there was a smile in her eyes. "Yes." She stroked the fur on the stuffed dog's head.

"Are you glad that Toni's going to be your step-mother?" he asked.

When she looked up again, her eyes glistened. "I miss Momma."

"I know, sweetheart. I wish your mom was still here."

"Is it wrong that I like Toni?" she asked, her voice small and unsure.

Zach stroked her head. "No, Lori, it isn't. I know your mom wanted to stay with you, but since she couldn't, I bet she's smiling down from heaven knowing that Toni loves you. And that you love her."

"Really?"

"Scout's honor."

Relief shone in her eyes. Zach only prayed that he was right.

Chapter 7

The noise in the Dallas airport had subsided, but Toni had the oddest feeling that she was being watched. She glanced up from her magazine to see her sister J.D. and her brother-in-law, Luke, bearing down on her. The expression on J.D.'s face told Toni she was in trouble—big time.

When Toni put the magazine down and stood, Zach looked at her, then saw the direction of her gaze.

"J.D., what are you doing here?" Toni asked, trying for a calm she didn't feel.

The expression on her sister's face was stern and nononsense. "I had an interesting conversation with a friend of mine this morning. Imagine my surprise, when Anna congratulated me on *your* upcoming marriage."

"Oh." Toni winced. When her engagement to Mark had gone sour, Toni had driven to J.D.'s house in Dallas and cried her eyes out. J.D. had tried to counsel her sister out of her bitterness, but Toni had vowed never again to put her heart on the line.

"Toni's going to be my momma," Lisa piped up, looking up at the adults.

Everyone's attention focused on the twins. Lori sat in her chair, silently studying the adults, while Lisa jumped to her feet and stood by Toni.

"Girls, you remember my sister, J.D. And this—" Toni pulled Luke forward "—is her husband, Luke."

After the greetings had been exchanged, J.D. pulled Toni into a bookstore across from the waiting area.

"What do you think you're doing?" J.D. softly demanded.

Toni tried for a calm which she wasn't feeling. "I'm going to get married."

"Since when did you change your mind about that institution?" J.D. demanded.

"Since I met the twins."

J.D.'s gaze roamed over Zach and the children. "He's using you, Toni. You do know that, don't you?"

"And I'm using him."

Surprise colored J.D.'s face. "You want to explain that statement to me?"

"Sis, I'm tired of Dad trying to set me up with men. Before Mom was killed, there must've been a different man each time I came home that Dad tried to set me up with." Visions of Carl danced through her brain. "And I'm also tired of hearing the ladies at the country club and church sighing over poor Toni, who couldn't keep a man."

"Ignore them."

Toni met her sister's eyes. "I have. But I can't walk away from the girls, J.D. They need me. And I can make a difference for them. And nothing you say will change my mind. I'd like some support from you.'' Her voice was filled with conviction.

"Have you told Dad?" J.D. asked.

"No."

J.D. shook her head. "There's going to be trouble, you know that?"

A sigh escaped Toni's mouth. "I know, but this is something I want to do."

J.D. hesitated.

"I have to do this," Toni added. She didn't understand why she needed to have J.D.'s support, but she was sure it would make a difference. J.D. had moved bigger mountains than their dad.

"All right, sis. You have my support." Her eyes narrowed. "And I'm sure glad you had that prenup agreement drawn up."

"That was Zach's idea," Toni admitted.

"Oh?" J.D. arched her brow. "Well, I won't tell Dad, but you won't mind if I call Alex and Rafe?"

"Fine, but warn them that I'm the one who needs to break the news to Dad."

"I don't think you'll have a problem getting your wish." Both sisters smiled at the remark. George's temper was legendary, and not many people tangled with him.

"Thanks," Toni whispered, wrapping her arms around her sister.

J.D. pulled back. "What else could I do for my baby sister? Good luck."

Toni sighed. Having J.D. on her side was a big break. It might make a difference in telling her dad. Then again, maybe nothing would.

The airplane dropped suddenly, causing passengers to gasp. Zach looked across the aisle to where Toni sat, flanked by his slumbering daughters. Both girls had succumbed to their exhaustion. It had been a monumental day for them. They were still asleep.

"What are you studying?" Toni asked.

"I had my secretary pull the service records on the field where we found the dead gauger."

"What are you looking for?"

"Yesterday I received reports from the field engineer that the reason the reserve tank had gone dry was the pump jack went out."

A frown gathered her brows. "Hadn't the field recently been serviced?"

"I'm impressed at your knowledge."

"Why? Have you forgotten who my dad is?"

That wouldn't happen any time soon. "You should've heard our dinner conversation about viscosity, saltwater, heater treaters, or dead birds in the sludge pit."

Zach shook his head. "According to this report, the field should have been serviced six weeks ago."

She frowned. "They should've caught the problem—if they actually did the work."

Zach's steely smile made Toni glad she wasn't the one responsible for the field.

"Ah, I see the problem."

He set aside his papers and changed the subject. "I take it that your sister wasn't too happy with your news."

Toni glanced down at the girls to make sure they were still asleep. "She wanted to assure herself everything was okay."

"Why would she worry?" he asked.

Toni gently brushed back the hair that fell on Lisa's

forehead. "I was engaged briefly a couple of years ago. When I walked in on my fiancé in bed with another woman, I took it—uh—badly. I hit him with his birthday cake."

He laughed. "He's lucky that's all you did."

Toni smiled. "That's why J.D. was surprised by my actions."

"That's understandable." Zach glanced down at his daughters. "Why did you agree, Toni?"

She wanted to tell him what motivated her, but she didn't want to give him that truth at the moment. It was too close to her heart. "Isn't it enough that I agreed?"

After studying her for a moment, he nodded. "Yes."

He went back to his reports. Toni closed her eyes and wondered if she had made a mistake. She prayed she hadn't.

"Is this the place where you're going to get married?" Lisa asked, glancing at the glittering signs of the Las Vegas wedding chapel. She had her face pressed to the back seat window. The building advertised instant weddings—everything that was needed for a complete ceremony.

They had checked in at the hotel, changed into wedding finery, then went looking for a chapel.

"Yes, Lisa, this is the place," Zach replied, shutting off the engine.

Zach glanced at Toni. "If you'll take Lisa, I'll get Lori."

"Divide and conquer, again?" Toni replied with a smile.

"You got it."

It took less than ten minutes for the ceremony to be arranged and the chapel to set things up.

"Smell my flowers," Lisa told Toni, holding up the daisies and baby's breath.

Lori held a similar bouquet. Each girl had on a new white dress with daisies scattered over it. Toni smiled at them and gave each child a hug.

Lori whispered, "I'm glad you're going to be my momma." The little girl grasped Toni's hand.

Tears welled in Toni's eyes. "I'm glad, too." And she meant every word.

Zach watched Lisa skip down the aisle, with Lori limping after her. His heart lurched. They were the reason he was here, he reminded himself. Then he saw Toni walking toward them, dressed in a simple cream suit, and suddenly he couldn't think of anything else.

Antonia Anderson was a beautiful woman. Her chin-length light brown hair swayed with each step, framing an elegant face and deep blue eyes. When her gaze met his, a hesitant smile curved her well-shaped mouth.

He couldn't think in those terms if he was going to keep his sanity. He should've learned his lesson with the twins' mother, but apparently he hadn't.

You're in trouble here. Remember what happened when you let your hormones rule your head, a voice in his head whispered.

Clamping down on his feelings, he turned to the minister.

The ceremony quickly passed. When he took Toni's hand and slipped on the plain gold band, his eyes met hers. Heat raced through him.

Her fingers trembled as she slipped a matching band onto his finger. As she started to release his hand,

Zach's other hand stopped her. Her startled gaze flew to his.

"I now pronounce you husband and wife. You may kiss the bride."

Zach only meant to give her a brief kiss. But as his mouth skimmed over hers, something changed. His lips molded to hers and felt her response in the clinging of her lips. He was tempted to deepen the kiss, to pull her flush against his body, when he felt a tug on his trouser leg.

"C'mon, Dad," Lisa complained. "We're hungry."

When he pulled back from Toni, he noted the softness in her eyes and knew she regretted having to stop as much as he did.

But it was better this way.

Zach looked down at Lisa. "So, you're hungry, are you?"

"Yeah, and I hafto go, too."

Zach's startled gaze flew to Toni's.

Biting back a grin, she said, "I'll take her."

As the girls walked to the rest room, the minister said, "Don't get discouraged. Children are a gift."

Zach glanced at the man. "They're a surprise, I grant you that."

"Enjoy the time when they're young," the minister added.

"I just hope I live through it."

"Wow, I liked the guys who flew in the air," Lisa chattered as they entered their hotel room.

"What did you like best about the circus, Lori?" Toni asked.

She gave Toni a shy smile. "I liked the elephants. When they danced, it was funny."

Lori yawned and from the drooping of her shoulders, Toni could tell she was at the end of her strength. "Okay, girls, let's get ready for bed."

Zach expected the girls to argue with Toni as they had done with him for the past few weeks. Instead, they nodded their heads and followed Toni into the bathroom. Zach stared after them, wondering what power Toni had that affected the girls that way.

When the twins were washed up and in their pj's, Zach helped Toni tuck them into bed.

"This has been a fun day," Lisa said as she snuggled beneath the covers.

"I'm glad you liked it," Toni replied.

"Yeah, I told Lori that if Dad married you, it would be good."

Zach studied his charming daughter, and a suspicion formed in his mind. All those housekeepers had been run off on purpose. Because they wanted him to marry Toni. No, that couldn't be. The girls were only four years old.

"Good night," Toni whispered to the girls and gave each a kiss.

The girls smiled at him. Zach leaned over and brushed a kiss across each forehead. This ritual had started the second night the girls had been with him. Lisa had demanded a kiss, just like Momma had done. Zach had felt like an Eskimo in the Amazon jungle, out of place and not knowing what to do next, so he'd brushed a kiss on each girl's forehead. From that time on, they had expected a kiss good-night. Each day, he felt less self-conscious.

"Thank you, Daddy, for getting us a mommy," Lisa whispered as she snuggled down into the covers. "I told Lori that you would."

Bingo, his suspicions were just confirmed. His daughters had suckered him. Zach's gaze met Toni's. Once in the living room, Zach turned to Toni.

"I think I've been the focus of a scam that my daughters have run," he quietly told her.

Silent laughter shook Toni. "Could be."

"They purposely ran off all those housekeepers."

"Sounds like it."

"But they're so young—"

"Zach, children are a lot smarter than most people think."

He rubbed his neck. "I guess you're right. Did you ever do something like that to your dad?" he asked.

"I'm afraid so. But as time went on, Dad grew better and better at detecting our scams, so by the time I tried pulling some stunts—the third and youngest daughter—he'd seen them twice before. But I heard stories from my older sisters."

Zach shook his head. "I guess I have a lot to learn."

She smiled at him. "I'll help you."

Electricity arced between them, setting Zach's blood to racing, and his mind wandered to thoughts of satin sheets and hot bodies. He looked at the couch.

"I can sleep in here," he said, feeling as if he were slowly drowning.

Toni's gaze went from the couch to the door to the girls' room. "Don't you think the girls will wonder why you're sleeping out here instead of in the bedroom?"

"I can get up before the girls," he reasonably replied.

Toni crossed her arms over her chest. "Zach, how many times during the past three weeks have the girls slept through the night?"

Already there was a flaw in his plans. "Most of the nights."

"But there's a chance that maybe one of the girls will wander through this room. And don't you think that they will question why you're sleeping out here on the couch? And if the court sends anyone to investigate our relationship, you wouldn't want the girls to say, 'Daddy slept in the living room the night he got married.' Remember, so far, the girls have been honest in their accounting of things."

He studied her. "The only other option is that I sleep in the same bed as you."

"We're adults, Zach. I think we can sleep in the same bed and not have a problem."

He wished he was as sure as she was. Finally, he nodded. "Why don't I wait here while you get ready for bed?"

Toni had only been gone for a few minutes when he heard, "Daddy?"

Zach looked up from the TV screen and saw Lori in the doorway. "What is it?"

"I'm thirsty," she said.

He stood and took Lori's hand. "Come on, let's get you a drink, then back to bed."

After she drank her water, Zach helped her back under the covers. Lori smiled at him, a beautiful full smile that shimmered in her eyes.

"Thank you, Daddy."

As he looked down at his daughter, Zach knew that she wasn't just thanking him for the water. His heart contracted. He brushed her cheek with his fingers and smiled. When he turned, he saw Toni standing in the doorway.

She moved into the living room and waited for him.

"She needed some water," he explained, turning off the TV.

Toni nodded but didn't say anything, which he appreciated. His ex-wife often and repeatedly had told him when he was wrong.

"The bathroom's yours," she said, then slipped into the bedroom.

When Zach followed her, his gaze went to the bed. It was only a full-size mattress. He cursed. Luck wasn't with him. Why couldn't it have been a king-size? Or queen? Or twin beds? He considered taking a pillow and blanket and stretching out on the floor, but Lori had proven Toni's argument true, and he didn't want the girls to find him there. The only option he had left was sleeping in the bed.

As he got ready for bed, Zach had to laugh at himself. Since when was he nervous about getting into bed with a beautiful woman? Since he'd promised not to touch her.

Turning off the bathroom light, he walked into the darkened bedroom. He gave himself enough time for his eyes to adjust to the darkness, then walked to the bed. He slipped off his shirt, shoes, then shucked off his pants. Usually, he slept nude, but since the girls had entered his life, he'd been leaving on his briefs.

Slipping under the covers, Zach became instantly aware of Toni lying not six inches from him. He heard each time she took a breath. So soft and appealing, making him want to roll over and cover her full mouth with his own. But if he did that, he wouldn't stop. He had given Toni his word that this marriage wouldn't include sex, and he wasn't going to break his word to her.

He needed to have his head examined, because he

couldn't think of anything more asinine than that promise he'd given her.

Gritting his teeth, he rolled onto his side, calling on all the training in self-discipline that he'd had to use as a Special Forces member, learning how to sleep in a tense situation.

How could he forget the lessons his failed first marriage had taught him? He was no good with this male-female thing. And what kind of example had his parents set for him? His father had been separated from his wife when he met Zach's mother. Their affair had been brief, and when his dad went back to his wife, he left Zach's mother pregnant and alone. Zach's mother had never forgiven his dad and held no love for her son, either.

So what made Zach think that he could have a successful relationship with Toni?

And although his mind told him things wouldn't work out, his body still craved her.

He cursed.

Toni tried to relax her muscles, but her body wouldn't obey her mind's commands. She knew exactly where Zach's body lay—inches from hers. She knew the temptation that the intimacy of marriage would present, but she hadn't counted on her body rebelling against her mind.

Remember the reason he married you, she told herself. It was so he could keep his children—nothing more.

She didn't worry that Zach would try to press her for sex, because he'd shown her before he wasn't interested. After he'd brought her home from that disastrous Christmas party, she had wanted to kiss him, offered him her lips. But Zach had politely stepped away from her, nodded goodbye and left. She had never felt so foolish in her life as she had watching Zach walk back to his car and drive away that night.

What worried Toni, as she lay next to him, is that she might ask him to love her. And she didn't think her heart could bear another rejection. Once was more than enough.

It was the heat that drew her. And the feeling of safety and peace. Toni rubbed her cheek over the surface. The pillow was hairy instead of smooth. Shock raced through her brain. A hairy pillow? Next, she became aware that her hand rested on warm skin stretched over hard muscle.

Her brows gathered into a frown. Slowly, she opened her eyes to see the gentle rise and fall of Zach's chest. She was curled close to his side, her hand splayed over his pectoral muscle and her leg was thrown over his.

Her skin sizzled with the contact. How could skin be so sensitive? Her fingers contracted negligibly.

Although the feeling of lying next to him was heavenly, this wasn't part of their bargain.

Toni's knee moved, trying to disengage her body from Zach's. A moan rumbled in his chest. Toni's gaze flew to his. Zach's green eyes glittered with passion. His hand, which rested on her hip, contracted.

"Uh..."

"Shh," he whispered. "Give me a moment."

Toni didn't dare move a muscle. With her ear on his chest, Toni heard the thundering of his heart. Hers was keeping pace with his. For two people who had simply entered this marriage as a business arrangement, things sure had gotten complicated. And quickly.

After he took a deep breath, his hand fell back onto the bed. Toni immediately sat up. The sheet fell to her waist and her nipples plainly showed through the thin fabric of her nightgown. Her state of arousal couldn't be hidden.

She scooted to the far side of the bed. "I'm sorry, Zach. When I woke, I was…"

He sat up and glanced at his position in the bed. "From the looks of things, I don't think you were the only person who moved during the course of the night."

He was right. Zach was in the center of the bed. Apparently, they had moved toward each other during the night.

Before she could respond, the girls appeared at the door.

"Hi," chirped Lisa. Zach covered himself before Lisa launched herself onto the bed. "We're hungry." She flopped on the bed.

Toni glanced at Zach. "Well, why don't I help you two get dressed while your daddy dresses? Then we'll have breakfast."

The girls yelled their approval. As she walked out of the bedroom, Toni's gaze brushed Zach's. The heat still shimmered there. And she felt it down to her toes.

Zach held his razor under the warm stream of water. As he looked to take a second swipe at his beard, he paused. Had he lost all his marbles? The memory of holding Toni in his arms this morning burned into his brain. How had they managed to get so entwined? He'd awakened minutes before Toni and tried to decide the best way to disengage himself from her, when Toni had snuggled against him like a kitten.

As he finished shaving, he remembered every exquisite inch of her. He had just decided to throw caution to the wind when Lisa had bounced into the room.

What was wrong with him? Had his common sense completely evaporated? He knew if he gave in to those pulsing hormones, then he was setting himself up for a fall.

Wiping off his face, Zach decided to clamp down on his feelings. He had enough trouble. He didn't need to invite any more.

"Couldn't we have stayed longer? I wanted to ride on that big round thing we saw at the hotel." Lisa turned to her father. The airplane had just taken off, flying back to Dallas.

"The Ferris wheel," Toni explained, as a frown appeared on Zach's brow.

"The reason we have to go home today is Toni has to go to school on Monday," he explained.

"Then we could've stayed until tomorrow," Lisa argued.

Smiling at her, Toni took Lisa's hand. "I have several things I have to do on Sunday to get ready for my classes. Also, I think your daddy has some work he has to do."

Lisa folded her arms across her chest and pouted.

Toni turned to Zach. "In our hurry to get here, we never decided where we were going to live. If you don't have any objection, why don't you and the girls move in with me? Since I have my aviary out in the backyard, it will make my life easier if I can stay put."

"What's an aviary?" Lisa asked.

Toni smiled. "It's a place for keeping birds confined."

"Why do you have one?" Lisa asked.

"Because I rescue sick and hurt birds and help them get well."

"Why?" Lisa asked.

"Because I teach people about birds and together we help wild animals." Toni looked at Zach.

"I don't have any objection to that. Once we land in Midland, we could stop by my apartment and pack the girls' and my things."

"Don't you think that will take several hours?" Toni asked.

"I can move my things in twenty minutes. The girls' might take a little longer than that."

Toni's eyes widened. "Don't you have any furniture or dishes or kitchen items?"

"No."

She hadn't realized how little Zach possessed. His clothes and his car. And he'd had to change his car since the girls came into his life.

"Well, then if that's all you'll need to do, I think we can get you moved in tonight."

He nodded.

"But today, if there's time, or tomorrow, Zach, we're going to have to go to my father's house and tell him about our marriage."

Zach's eyes locked with hers. From his expression, Zach knew that job would be formidable.

"Can we get Sam?" Lori asked.

Toni looked at Lori. In all the time she'd been with the little girl, she hadn't heard her ask for anything but Sam.

Swallowing, Toni said, "We'll try."

Zach hadn't misjudged the time it would take them to pack up everything in the apartment. Within thirty

minutes all of Zach's and the girls' things were packed.
As Toni walked into the living room, she saw the
empty fishbowl on the bookcase and recalled Zach's
story about the garden burial.

"Do you want to bring your fishbowl?" Toni asked
the girls.

"I liked the fishies, but they kept dying." Lisa
frowned.

Toni squatted down and pushed the hair back from
Lisa's forehead. "Well, why don't we put it in the car
and maybe this week we could buy some more fish."

"'Kay."

Toni looked around. "Did we forget anything else?"

"Yeah, the Froot Loops," Lisa added.

Toni glanced at Zach.

Zach explained, "The girls took me to the grocery
store. It's an interesting place."

From the look on his face, she'd just bet it had been
an experience for him.

"We picked up a few things that the girls liked."

Nodding, Toni walked into the kitchen and opened
several of the cabinets. She found the foodstuffs, and
packed them in a couple of grocery sacks.

There was an odd collection of dishes in the cabinet.
When she started to pack them, he said, "Leave
them."

"There's nothing you want? Maybe the girls have
something they'd like to keep?"

"After four weeks?" he asked.

"Sure. Lisa, Lori, are there any of these dishes you
want to keep?"

"Yeah, I want the doggie glass," Lisa said.

"I want my Big Bird spoon," Lori added.

A blush crept up Zach's throat. When his gaze met hers, he shrugged. "They saw the stuff when we went to the store. It helped."

First the empty fishbowl and now the special gifts. Zach may not have had any ideas on how to care for children when he picked up the girls four weeks ago, but he had made amazing progress. The wall Toni had built around her heart took another big hit. Oh, she was in trouble here.

"Let me pack these things, then why don't we drop by my dad's house and tell him the news?"

Leaning against the counter, Zach studied her. "Want to get it over with, huh?"

Toni studied the spoon on the counter. "In spite of Dad's gruff demeanor, he's always been a good father. When I was in the accident, he went to great lengths to make sure I'd have the best care. Of course, all of us girls discovered early on that his bark was worse than his bite."

"Well, I wouldn't spread it around at work. I think your dad enjoys his status of being a mean SOB."

Laughing, Toni agreed. "I worked for dad, remember? In the billing office. I know how he values his reputation. I won't ruin it."

She tried to hold on to that thought as they headed for the car.

Chapter 8

When they stopped in front of her dad's front door, Toni frowned at the number of cars parked in the circular drive.

"What's wrong?" Zach asked. Her reaction made him nervous. He knew this meeting with George was going to be hard, but it had to be done. He'd agreed with Toni that it should be done as quickly as possible.

"The cars in the drive," Toni replied.

Zach looked at them. "So?"

Toni turned to him. "It appears that my entire family is here."

That was a bad sign. He glanced again at the collection of vehicles. "You think your sister told everyone else about your wedding?"

"I'm sure she did, so be prepared to smile and be charming."

His eyes widened. "What do you mean?"

"Don't give them your stony-faced military man

pose, Zach. It probably won't affect the men of the group, who are all lawmen themselves and know how to do their own scowling. But smile at my sisters. They'll be your best allies.''

"Allies? You make it sound like war."

Her brow arched. "You're perceptive."

If her other sister was as tough a case as J.D., he was going to have to use all the charm he could muster. As for the lawmen, J.D had already warned him about them. Well, there was nothing to do about it except dive in.

They hadn't reached the front door when it was thrown open and Alex, Toni's other sister, came running out. Zach knew all these people by sight because he'd seen their pictures in George's office countless times, but he'd never managed to be around to be introduced to them.

"Toni," Alex cried, wrapping her sister in a big hug. "How are you?" Pulling back, Alex critically eyed Toni from head to foot. "You look wonderful." Her gaze went to Zach, and she smiled.

Lori stepped close to Zach and grasped his hand. It was the first time his daughter had ever reached out to him. A lump formed in his throat.

"Do you want to introduce me?" Alex looked at the girls, then him.

"Sis," Rafe called from the door. "Why don't you let Toni come inside, then she can introduce them to her entire family instead of the neighborhood."

"All right." She waved him off. "He sure has become bossy. Come on, everyone, the family's waiting."

It had an ominous sound to it.

The entire Anderson family was gathered in the den.

J.D. and her husband, Luke, and their two children; Alexandra and her husband, Derek, and their two daughters; and finally Rafe and his wife, April, who was expecting. And George, the head of the family.

They were a formidable group, but Zach had faced worse odds.

"Are they all your family?" Lisa whispered to Toni. The awe in his daughter's voice made Zach want to smile.

"Yes, sweetie, they are," Toni answered softly.

Lisa's gaze returned to the group. "Wow. And are they now mine, too?" she whispered again.

His daughter's question revealed how lonely the child had been. And Zach could identify with that feeling of isolation. He'd grown up with it.

"Yes, they are," Toni said, bending low so her family wouldn't hear. Lisa's smile lit the room.

As quickly as possible, Toni introduced everyone. She didn't mention what had happened yesterday. She wanted the girls in the other room when she told everyone.

"Well, Toni, I expect you have news for us, don't you?" George said after the children had gone to the game room to play video games. He sat in a large leather chair beside the fireplace.

Toni glanced at J.D., who silently shook her head.

"No one spilled the beans, Toni," George added, seeing the exchange. "But when your sisters and brother suddenly showed up, it wasn't hard to figure out something was up. When I couldn't get hold of you...by means of simple deduction that meant you were the news. So tell me, what is it?"

Toni opened her mouth, but Zach couldn't let her be

the one to walk into the lion's den by herself. He said, "Toni and I flew to Vegas and got married yesterday."

The room went deathly quiet, rather like the calm at the center of a hurricane. All eyes were trained on George, waiting.

He studied Toni. "I thought you didn't want to get married after that fiasco of an engagement you had. You haven't been too receptive to the men I've lined up for you."

"Dad," J.D. interjected, "we all know you meant well, but Toni wanted to pick her own husband, like the rest of us."

"And I can just imagine who you lined up, Dad," Alex offered. She shivered. "I had several dates that you arranged."

George's eyes narrowed as he studied his youngest. "That so?"

Toni walked over to her father and sat on the footstool in front of his chair. "Dad, you've always been there for me, particularly after my accident, pushing me and helping me. But I'm a grown woman now, and I want to live my own life. And who I marry is my choice."

George's gaze clashed with Zach's. "And he's who you want?" he demanded.

Glancing over her shoulder, Toni's eyes softened as they rested on him. Zach read a momentary tenderness there. She faced her father. "Yes."

That simple word shot through Zach like a 220 current, electrifying every cell in his body. Damn. Zach felt about an inch tall when faced with Toni's reaction. He'd married again only to keep custody of the girls. Nothing more.

Liar, a voice in his head yelled.

George smiled at his child. "If that's what you want, then you have my blessings." Toni went into her father's arms. Over his daughter's shoulder, Zach read the message in the old man's eyes. *If you hurt her, I'll make you sorry.*

It seemed that the spectators were released from the invisible bonds that held them, and they each came by to congratulate Zach.

Luke was the first to shake Zach's hand. "Don't worry about George. He's very protective of his daughters. We've all run the gauntlet. But you would understand that, since you have two little girls of your own."

Zach was only beginning to understand and appreciate George's feelings for his daughters. And in spite of things, Zach couldn't blame the older man for his attitude.

He just hoped he would survive the experience.

George and Zach walked into the study and closed the door behind them.

"What have you found out about the oil field mess?" George asked him.

The question stunned Zach. He had prepared himself for George's explosive temper. He didn't quite know what to make of this approach. He'd expected his new father-in-law to talk to him about his marriage to Toni.

"I had my secretary pull the service records on that field," Zach began. "It should've been serviced six weeks ago. Accounting has a paid invoice for the work."

"So, what's bothering you about it?" George asked, leaning back in his chair.

"If they did the work, then why did the pump jack burn out when it had another six months to replacement? When I got reports back from the investigator about the equipment, they stated that it looked like the jack hadn't been serviced in a long time."

"So, there's something rotten in this entire mess," George mused.

"I think so. I have a feeling this isn't the only incident. We're going to need to look into it. I plan to send another engineer out to look at all the fields that Caprock has worked on."

"Good idea," George added. "I've got some figures on crude that's gone to the refinery, and it doesn't match the figures that should've been pumped."

Zach rubbed his neck. The situation was going from bad to worse.

"Sure looks like it." George studied the man before him. "I like you, Zachary Knight. You saved my bacon from those terrorists when we were in Venezuela. And I wanted to pay you back. But—" George pinned Zach with a steely-eyed expression "—that didn't include my daughter."

"I—"

George held up his hand. "Toni's special. If you hurt her, Zach, I'll make you sorry you were born. Understand?" George's voice held a chill.

Zach looked into the steady eyes of the old man. Just because George Anderson wasn't in his prime, it didn't mean the man couldn't hire someone to beat Zach to a pulp.

"Toni's a beautiful, generous and kind woman, George. The last thing I want to do is hurt her."

George nodded. "Good, then we understand each other."

"We do. And if you're worried about her inheritance, I signed a prenuptial agreement with her. I'll never make any claim on her money.''

"You're a smart man. Then let's go and join the others. I know my daughters are worried that I might shoot you and hide the body in the nearest dry hole.''

Zach didn't doubt that his daughters' worry was well-founded.

As they walked back to the living room, Zach hoped that he hadn't—no wouldn't—hurt Toni. Not because of George's threats. No, because wounding that beautiful woman was the last thing he wanted to do.

Toni breathed a sigh of relief when Zach and her father walked back into the room.

"He's still alive,'' J.D. whispered to her sister. "That's an encouraging sign.''

Glaring at her sister, Toni murmured, "I wonder what Dad chatted with Zach about?''

"Do you really want to know?''

Toni frowned. "Of course.'' She walked over to where all the men stood. "Do you mind if I borrow my father?'' she asked the group.

When no one objected, Toni pulled her father into the backyard. "All right, Dad, spill the beans. What did you say to Zach?''

"We talked company business.''

"And?''

"And what?'' He tried to look innocent and shocked, but she didn't buy the routine. "What makes you think we talked about anything else?''

"Because I spent a lifetime observing you, watching how you handled J.D.'s and Alex's marriages.'' She met his gaze. "Did you threaten him?''

"Toni, the man's an ex-soldier. I wouldn't be fool

enough to challenge him. I simply told him to make sure he did right by you, and that I'd be watching."

It was beyond Toni to get mad at her father. They'd gone through so much together, her accident, her mother's death, that she couldn't resent his interference. But that didn't mean she had to sanction his interference, either. "Dad, this is a choice I've made," she repeated her earlier point. "I want you to respect that."

He rubbed his neck. "I do, I do. Now, why don't we go back inside and join the others?"

As they walked into the house, Toni felt as if she'd just spit into the wind.

Zach looked out the sliding glass doors and watched Toni and George on the patio.

"Don't worry about her," J.D. told Zach, following the direction of his gaze. "Dad has a tender spot for his youngest. Besides, if any of us could talk Dad into our way of thinking, it was Toni."

Zach's brow arched. "I didn't think anyone changed your father's mind once it was made up."

"It's been known to have happened. Toni and her mom were probably the only two people who could accomplish the feat."

He nodded.

"Of course, Toni might intercede for you with Dad, but I want you to know, if you hurt my sister, I'll make you sorry."

Zach turned and stared at J.D. She was a chip off the old block.

"J.D., what are you saying to this man?" Luke, her husband, asked.

"We were simply exchanging congratulations." She smiled, clasped her husband's arm and walked away.

Zach knew he should be insulted, but he couldn't prevent the smile that curved his lips. Apparently, his new wife had some very staunch defenders.

How would it feel to have someone love you so much they'd risk it all for you?

"Daddy, I like my new family." Lisa sat up in her bed. "There were so many kids to play with." Her eyes shone with excitement. "And I have a grandpa and aunts and uncles and cousins."

"And are you happy, too, Lori?"

She smiled. "Auntie Alex told me all about Toni's time in a cast and how she didn't like it. Auntie Alex also told me how to take care of my cast."

"And we get to have Sam come live with us," Lisa chirped in.

When George had said that Sam could come home with them as a wedding present, the girls had gone crazy with elation.

Toni walked out of the bathroom, where she'd been straightening up after the girls' bath.

Lisa smiled at her. "I'm glad we visited Grandpa. It was neat."

"I'll tell him that you think he's neat."

"Naw, all the people were neat," Lisa commented. "I like having cousins."

Toni settled the girls under the covers and after both Zach and Toni kissed the children, they walked into the living room.

"Toni, we need to talk," Zach said.

She turned to him. "About what?"

"Our sleeping arrangements."

"Why don't we go into the kitchen, and have something to drink. We don't want the girls overhearing us."

He nodded.

Toni got each of them a soft drink and she set a tin of homemade chocolate chip cookies in the center of the table. She pushed the open tin toward him. He took one look, grabbed a cookie and bit into it.

"Did you make these?" he asked.

She nodded.

She made a mean cookie. Damn. He didn't need to know any more of her virtues when he was already in over his head and sinking.

"What happened this morning when we woke up like we did was an—"

"Accident," she supplied.

The corner of his mouth kicked up. If that was an accident, he didn't want to encounter their conscious actions. "I guess that's the best way to describe it. But it can't happened again."

She looked wounded and relieved at the same time.

"If this thing—a platonic relationship—is to work, then we'll have to be more careful."

"So what exactly are you saying, Zach? Are you asking for separate bedrooms?"

"That would be the easiest way, but I think until the custody hearing, we shouldn't give the court any reason to doubt our marriage."

She frowned. "Then what are you suggesting?"

"I was wondering what kind of bed you have in your room. By any chance, you wouldn't have twin beds?" He couldn't prevent the hopeful note in his voice.

"No, I don't. But my mattress is a king. That will give us plenty of room."

Well, if he couldn't have a separate bed, at least he would have the most room between them that modern bedding could provide. He thought of sleeping in the third bedroom, or a daybed in her room if she had one, or even on the floor, but that left them in the same position as before, vulnerable to prying eyes and his sister-in-law's lawsuit. And he wasn't going to lose.

He took the last swig of his drink. "Why don't you show me where I need to put my things?"

She pursed her lips. "I didn't clear out any room in my dresser, but it won't take long for me to do that."

Zach followed her down the hall into her bedroom. He had his hanging bag over one shoulder and his nylon tote in the other hand.

Toni's bedroom was large, with French doors that led out onto a patio. The main color in the room was peach, with green and yellow accents. Her bed was one of those massive things with a mirror in the headboard and drawers and shelves on either side.

Opening the closet, she pushed aside her things for him to hang his suits. "How many drawers do you think you'll need?"

"One is plenty."

She gave him a skeptical look, then gathered her sweaters from a drawer in the dresser. "I'll put these in the spare room."

While she was gone, Zach unloaded his bag. He set his shaving kit in the bathroom. Bottles of colored something or other sat on the counter. He lifted the top of one cut crystal perfume bottle and smelled it. The fragrance was delicate and floral, reminding him of Toni.

Although her room and bathroom were overwhelmingly feminine, it was oddly comforting to Zach. By the time he returned to the bedroom, Toni stood by the bed frowning.

"What's wrong?" he asked.

"Do you want the first chance at the bathroom, or should I go first?"

"Why don't you go first?" Zach replied. "While you're doing that, I thought I'd check the doors and windows."

She gave him an odd look, then shrugged and went into the bathroom. For Zach, securing the perimeter was always something he wanted to do while on a mission. It had spilt over into his personal life by making sure that all the doors and windows were secure.

As he finished up his tour of the house, he stopped in the doorway of the girls' room. Sam, who had hopped up on the bed and stretched out between the girls, lifted his head. Zach smiled and shook his head. The changes one month had brought to his life were stunning. Sometimes he wondered if he had fallen into an alternate universe, where nothing was as it seemed, and he was groping to find his balance.

The harder he fought fate, the farther he slipped down into that open pit of no return. What was wrong with him?

As he walked into Toni's bedroom, she was coming out of the bathroom, wrapped in a soft, body-hugging robe that made Zach remember exactly what she felt like in his arms this morning.

She smiled at him, and the sight of her, freshly washed and glowing, her figure clearly outlined by the thin fabric of her gown and robe, nearly knocked him to his knees.

"I'm done in the bathroom. It's yours."

He nodded, praying that he had the strength to make

it through the night. Several of the missions that he'd gone on in Special Forces were looking like picnics in the park compared to the torture he was about to endure.

Toni glanced at Zach, who sat next to her in the pew. He'd had the oddest expression on his face when she started to get the girls ready for church. When she asked him to accompany them, he looked as if she'd asked him to jump over the house. After she'd explained it would probably be the easiest way to introduce their marriage to the community, she didn't have any problems. He'd reluctantly agreed to come with her.

The surprise on several longtime members' faces made Toni want to smile.

Lisa squirmed on the pew next to Toni.

"Are we finished, yet?" Lisa whispered in the dead silence after the sermon. Several heads turned.

Toni glanced at Zach, whose expression said she'd asked for this by bringing them. Her father, who sat beside them, choked back a laugh. Other members of her family shifted with their silent chuckles.

"Let's sing our final song," the choir director announced.

"Good." Lisa's voice rang through the church.

Once outside the building, several church members came by to say hello, and Toni introduced her new family to them. Through the crowd of people, Carl Ormand made his way toward them.

"What a surprise." His voice always had a nasal quality to it. "I've never seen you here, Knight."

"I didn't know this was an exclusive club, Ormand.

I thought the church was open to everyone,'' Zach countered.

Carl's eyes narrowed. Before he could reply, George Anderson appeared by Toni's side.

''Ah, Carl, are you here to congratulate my daughter on her marriage?'' he asked.

''To whom?''

''Our head of security, Zach. And I believe that Toni is thrilled with the girls.''

Through gritted teeth, Carl offered his best wishes, then quickly departed.

Toni and Zach exchanged a knowing glance, remembering the Christmas party where Carl had made a fool of himself, and Toni had first realized she was attracted to Zach.

''C'mon, Toni, bring your new family to lunch. We'll inform Zach of the family traditions he's going to have to live up to.''

After George walked away, Zach leaned closed. ''Am I going to like this?''

''Probably not.''

''That's what I was afraid of.''

Zach glanced at the reports his secretary had placed on his desk. Before he'd left on Friday, Zach had asked for all the service records of the company that worked on the field that blew up. From the papers, the company had done a lot of business with Anderson.

Looking at the address of the service company, The Caprock Service Company, Zach frowned. They were using a street address plus a suite number. He pulled out the phone book and looked for the company's listing. There was none.

Writing the address from the invoice on a piece of

paper, Zach stuck it in his pocket and locked up his office. He'd spent longer than he intended looking at the records. He felt guilty for hurrying Toni and the girls away from the Anderson estate this afternoon, but he wanted to check out this report.

As he strode toward the elevators, Carl Ormand walked out of his office. "Zach, what are you doing here?" A note of surprise colored his voice. "And so soon after your marriage? Didn't you want to spend time with your new bride?"

Zach pinned the man with a hard stare. "I think your mother did a poor job of teaching you manners, Ormand. But if you continue to ask personal questions, I can demonstrate what's appropriate."

Carl's eyes narrowed. He didn't say anything but turned around and went back into his office.

Zach had an uneasy feeling between his shoulders about Ormand. What was the man doing here on Sunday? Zach could understand Carl's attitude about his marriage to Toni—sour grapes were never easy to swallow—but why was he here today?

Zach got in his car and drove to the address listed on the invoice. The billing address for the Caprock Services was a private mail center. Staring at the building, Zach decided that first thing tomorrow he would call the phone number on the invoice and see if he could track down Caprock.

When he drove into the driveway of Toni's house, he noticed a rental car parked in front. As he pulled out the house key Toni gave him before he left, the front door opened and his ex-sister-in-law, Melanie, appeared.

"Zach," Toni said from behind Melanie. "I called

your office, but you must have left. Melanie's wanting to talk to you."

Narrowing his eyes, Zach studied his ex-sister-in-law. "Why don't we go inside and talk?"

The woman glared at Zach, then turned and walked into the living room. Melanie clenched her teeth so hard, Zach was surprised that she didn't break her jaw.

"Daddy," Lisa yelled. "Look, Auntie Melanie is here. Did ya know she played with me and Sam? I told her all about our new family. Uncles, aunties and the other kids."

Zach looked at his other daughter. She sat on the sofa, her fingers wrapped around Sam's collar. He worried about what Melanie would say in front of the children and turned to Toni.

"Could we use your office to talk?"

"Of course. The girls and I will finish setting the table for dinner."

Once the door to the study was closed, Melanie turned and struck like a snake. "If you think that this sham marriage is going to work, then think again, Zachary Knight. You were never there for the girls. My sister had to raise those girls alone."

Resting his shoulder against the door, he replied, "And the only reason that she had to do that is because she never, ever told me about the twins." His words were soft, hard and cold.

Melanie tried to act surprised. "I don't believe that." Her bluff didn't work.

"Believe what you want, Melanie. But we both know that Sylvia hated me. And not telling me was part of her revenge. That was why we divorced when we did, before we had children. I guess we were a little late."

"You were a poor husband to Sylvia. And I don't doubt you'll be a rotten father, too. I know my sister would've wanted me to have the twins."

"Then why didn't you come forward after the accident that killed her?" he asked.

"That's none of your business. All you need to know is that I want the girls." Tears welled in her eyes.

"They are my daughters, Melanie, and I won't give them up without a fight." He stepped away from the door and opened it.

"Don't worry, Zach. That's exactly what I intend to give you."

Zach folded his arms behind his head and stared at the bedroom ceiling. Toni was next to him in the bed and he felt every inch of her luscious form. On the drive from the office earlier, he'd managed to convince himself that it wouldn't matter if he slept in the spare bedroom tonight to save his sanity. That was before Melanie had blown his plan to hell.

This day had been endless, with highs and lows that he hadn't expected.

"What did she say?" Toni's voice pierced the darkness.

Turning his head, he replied, "She threatened to take Lisa and Lori. Did she say anything to you?"

"No. When she appeared at the doorway, the girls instantly recognized her, and it seemed rude not to invite her inside. Your old apartment manager gave her the new address. Melanie seemed surprised when Lisa announced I was her new mother, and we had all just returned from Las Vegas. She didn't mention the custody battle to the girls."

He shook his head. "I bet Melanie didn't like the fact that we were married."

"She asked the girls how long they'd known me."

Turning onto his side, he propped his head on his hand. "And what did they say?"

"They told her that I helped them when they first came to Midland. That you weren't very good to start off, but that you were better now."

A chuckle escaped him. "And what did she say to that?"

"What could she say? When I asked how she found you, she mentioned that the social worker in Phoenix told her. She asked if you had received any court papers yet, and I told her she had to ask you."

He reached out and squeezed her hand. "Thanks, Toni." He wanted to pulled her under him and taste those incredible lips again and her neck and breasts—

Whoa! Common sense reared its ugly head in the nick of time. Instead, he released her hand and turned onto his back.

"Have you gotten a lawyer, Zach, to represent you in the court hearing, yet?" Toni asked.

"No. The man I talked to at Anderson told me he did corporate law, not family."

"Well, why don't you consider Anna Nunez? She's a good family lawyer and she seemed very receptive when we were in her office the other day. I could call her tomorrow and see if she has some time so we could stop by and see her."

The idea of having the same attorney who drew up the prenuptial agreement handle the custody hearing appealed to him. Besides, he liked the woman's efficiency. "That sounds good."

"Then I'll call her." After a moment she added, "Good night, Zach."

He returned the sentiment, but he knew it wasn't going to be a good night, when his body ached for hers.

Chapter 9

"So, you're telling me that you didn't know of the girls' existence until a month ago?" Anna asked Zach. Her gaze, like a laser, penetrated his.

"That's right. Sylvia and I met one weekend when I was on leave from my unit. There was instant attraction and we married as soon as the military allowed. But Sylvia and I had nothing in common but s—uh—lust." He shrugged. "And after a while we didn't even have that." Zach glanced at Toni. He hadn't told her the circumstances of his first marriage.

"We decided to call it quits before we had any children," he added. "When we split up, neither of us knew about her pregnancy."

Anna's brow raised with a question. "Are you sure the girls are yours?"

"My thoughts reflected yours, and when I left for Phoenix, I wanted a blood test to make sure the girls were mine. But the instant I saw Lisa and Lori, I knew the truth. They are the spitting image of my mother.''

''Did you have the blood test run?'' Anna asked.

''I did and got the results this week. It confirms what I knew—the girls are mine.''

Anna rested her elbows on her desk. ''Why do you want them, Mr. Knight? Don't you think the girls would be better with their aunt and her husband?''

''No, I don't, Ms. Nunez,'' he replied, his voice firm and commanding.

She didn't appear intimidated. ''And why is that?''

''Because I know what it feels like to be rejected by your father. I was a bastard, the product of an affair between a married man and my mother. He was separated from his wife when the affair happened. When my mom announced she was pregnant, my dad went back to his wife. He never wanted anything to do with me. Never acknowledged me in the little rural Texas town where we lived. I vowed to myself I'd never abandon any child I fathered. And to my dying breath, I plan to fight for my children.''

There was nothing like pulling all one's skeletons out of the closet and putting them on parade for the world to see. He glanced at Toni to see her reaction. Her eyes weren't filled with shock and revulsion, like Sylvia's had been. No, Toni's expression was full of compassion…and admiration.

Anna leaned back in her chair. ''You've convinced me, Mr. Knight.'' She glanced at Toni. ''It's my guess that you knew all this before you two were married.''

Toni nodded. ''Yes, I knew Zach wanted to marry me to keep his daughters. And I'm with him to achieve that goal. And, may I add, it was Zach who wanted to draw up the prenuptial agreement that we signed.''

A new light entered Anna's eyes as she studied Zach. "All right, Mr. Knight. You've hired yourself a lawyer."

Zach reached into his coat pocket and withdrew the letter he'd received from Melanie's lawyers. "I received this notification last Wednesday." He handed her the letter.

After scanning it, she made a copy of the letter and gave him the original. "I'll contact the attorneys listed here, then get back to you."

"Do you think she has any legal ground to stand on?" he asked.

"Sure she does. But you have the better position. Since your wife never told you of the girls' existence, you can't be faulted. You acted reasonably from the time you knew of their existence. The odds are in your favor."

"Good."

With a final handshake, they left the office. Zach walked Toni to her car. He wanted to say something about the ugly facts that he'd just revealed in the lawyer's office.

"I hope I didn't shock you with my stories of my ex-wife and parents."

Toni faced him. "You weren't responsible for your parents' actions."

The tension gripping him eased. "But everyone in that little town knew about my folks," he replied.

"Do you want to compare shocking stories, Zach?" she asked, leaning back against her car.

His brow wrinkled in a frown.

"You want to hear mine?"

He couldn't imagine what she had to say. "Sure."

Toni crossed her arms under her breasts. "My dad always wanted a boy."

"And he got one."

"But he didn't know about Rafe until last year, when he showed up and surprised us all. My dad grew up in the Valley and didn't know that the sweetheart he'd left behind had a baby."

She shook her head. "At the age of twenty, my dad moved to Midland, determined to make it rich. He worked in the oil fields, then decided to strike out on his own. He became a wildcatter. When he ran out of money, he married the daughter of the local banker. He got his money and later a daughter, my sister, J.D., from that marriage. Years went by, but Dad didn't get the son he wanted. So he had an affair with his secretary—my mother. He divorced his first wife and married my mother. She gave him two more daughters."

Apparently the Anderson family had some unsavory skeletons in their closet, also.

"The entire community knew what had happened. J.D.'s mom didn't handle the divorce well. She became an alcoholic. So, Zach, we all know about shame and being put on public display."

Zach wondered at her reaction. "And all that doesn't bother you?"

Shock crossed her face. "Sure it does. I wish my father hadn't done what he did. But my dad poured himself into his three daughters. J.D. tried to be the son my dad didn't have until recently. As for Alex and me, Dad was always there, pushing us to be the best we could be.

"When I broke my legs in that crash, it was Dad's will that brought me through that crisis. He never gave up." A tear misted in her eye. "Last year when Dad and Mother were in the crash that killed her, I worried about Dad. He seemed to give up the will to live. When he started to push men at me, again, trying to arrange a husband for me, it was a relief. He was back.''

Apparently, George Anderson had a bit of history himself.

''I can pick the girls up this afternoon, Zach, after my class,'' Toni told him. Both Toni and Zach had gone to the day-care center this morning and notified the school of the change in the girls' lives.

''All right. I have to run down some problems we're having.''

''Something to do with the incident in field number one the other day?''

''Yeah, it does. I need to check out Caprock. Their billing address was one of those mailbox franchises. I need to track them down.''

''I'll try to have dinner ready about six-thirty.''

With the exception of his time in the military, for the first time in his memory, someone had told him when to show up for dinner. ''I'll be there.''

Zach stared down at the phone number for Caprock. He tried it again, and the same little old lady answered the phone. He hung up without saying anything. The woman had told him she'd had that number since 1954.

He walked down to Carl's office. Carl was in charge of servicing all the fields.

''Carl, I tried to call the number on this invoice from Caprock. I got an Eda May Stonehouse and she informed me that the number on this invoice is hers and has been hers since the mid-fifties. What do you know about Caprock?''

Carl sat back in his chair. ''They've worked for us

for the past eighteen months. I haven't had any problem with them.''

"Have you ever been to their offices?" Zach asked.

"No. They've done their work. I didn't need to hold their hands.''

Carl's attitude stunk.

"Who recommended them to us?" Zach wanted a name and he wanted a body he could question.

"Our field manager."

"Which field manager?" Zach asked.

"Ollie Townshed."

"Well, why don't you have Ollie call me. I want to talk to him about Caprock," Zach ordered.

"Sure. I'll get a message out to him. It might be tomorrow before he can get back to you."

That wasn't unusual. "No problem." Zach left the office and went back to his own. He checked Caprock's account in the computer to see how often the company had serviced fields for them. Thirty entries over the past year and a half, worth forty thousand dollars. That seemed excessive. He printed out the data.

He wondered if the work Caprock had claimed had actually been done. He called George and told him of his suspicions. George agreed with him, that the fields needed to be checked. He'd hire an engineer to do that work.

Glancing at his watch, Zach noted that he needed to leave for home. Toni and the girls were waiting for him. The thought sent a shaft of warmth through him.

Toni and the girls had just finished putting the last of the dishes on the table, when Zach pulled into the driveway.

"Daddy's here," Lisa cried, going to the front door.

Sam barked his welcome and Toni heard the girls offer their welcome. Zach's deep voice rumbled a greeting.

"Hurry, Daddy, we're hungry," Lisa added.

Toni turned in time to see the twins dragging Zach into the kitchen-dining area. She grinned at the sight of the two little girls tugging on their father. When her eyes met his, a charge of awareness raced through her body. The more she was around Zach, the more in tune her body seemed to be to his.

"We made chicken and dumplin's," Lisa informed him. "We got to help make this funny green Jell-O, didn't we Lori?"

Lori nodded her head.

"They did help," Toni affirmed.

Zach had an odd look in his eyes as he took in the scene before him, almost as if he couldn't believe what he was seeing. Suddenly, it occurred to Toni that maybe Zach had rarely had this kind of experience of coming home and finding his family and a dinner waiting for him.

Her eyes met his. And for an instant Toni felt she saw straight into his soul.

"Dad, I got to stir the hot water into the Jell-O," Lisa continued, snagging their attention.

During the meal, the twins told Zach about their venture into cooking. He listened and asked questions.

"And are you going to cook tomorrow night?" he asked the girls.

The girls looked at Toni. "I'll need help tomorrow, too," she reassured them.

"Goody."

"And, I'm going to need help after dinner cleaning up," Toni added.

"Daddy can help, then," Lisa informed them.

Toni shook her head. The child was bright, inventive and a handful. "Since we all ate, I think it's fair if we all help clean up."

"Oh."

Zach smiled. "I think that's a wonderful idea. Don't you, Lisa?"

She pursed her lips. "Yes."

Zach winked at Toni and her heart skipped a beat. This was too close to the real thing of a normal husband and wife, who married because they loved each other. Toni needed to remember their deal. They were using each other.

Her head might know that, but her heart wasn't co-operating.

Zach listened to the girls giggle as they took their bath. Sam barked, then another burst of laughter followed.

"Catch him, Zach," he heard Toni yell. An instant later, a wet, soapy Sam ran through the kitchen. Zach leaned over and snagged the dog's collar.

Sam dripped water onto the kitchen floor. Toni momentarily appeared at the door and threw Zach a towel.

"Dry him off before he tracks water throughout the house." She raced back to the bathroom.

Sam's sad eyes looked at him while Zach dried the animal. "What happened in there, boy?"

"He decided to join the girls in the tub," Toni yelled from the other room.

"It was fun, too, Daddy," Lisa added.

Zach frowned at the dog. "You better not have fleas."

The girls appeared at the doorway. "We're ready for bed. Can Sam join us?"

"Not until he's dry," Toni told the girls.

"Oh."

"Later, I'll bring him into your room," Toni informed them.

"C'mon, Dad, help tuck us in."

As Zach followed them into the bedroom, he marveled at the changes in his life this past month. From being alone and unconnected, he was now a father, husband and the proud owner of a golden retriever, which George was kind enough to let the girls have.

It still stunned him.

Zach sat at the kitchen table, studying some sort of a report.

"Would you like another slice of cake or something to drink?" Toni asked. She rested her hands on the top of a chair.

"Are you trying to fatten me up?" he asked.

She glanced at his slim waist. No, she didn't want to do that. She liked him far too much just the way he was. And that was the problem. She was falling under his spell as she watched him struggle to respond to the girls. "I wanted some iced tea. I thought if you wanted something, I'd get it for you."

A slow seductive smile curved his mouth. "I'd like some cake and tea. Can I help?"

"Sure. You're going to need to know your way around the kitchen. I'll show you where things are."

As they worked together, she asked, "What were you looking at?"

He eyed her, made some sort of decision and said,

"I pulled the records on Caprock Service Company. They've done a lot of business with Anderson Oil."

She put the plates on the table. "So?"

"In the past year and a half, we've paid them close to forty thousand dollars."

Toni's head snapped up. "That's a mighty big amount. How often and how many fields have they serviced?"

"That's what I was checking. Do you have any idea what the normal fee would be for servicing the field and how often?"

Toni couldn't prevent her laughter. Zach gave her a puzzled frown. "Zach, I paid those bills the entire time I worked for Dad. I'll be happy to look at them."

As they ate their cake, Toni reviewed Caprock's account, checking how many fields they supposedly serviced and which ones. Finally, after forty minutes, she sat back.

"It appears to me that a scam has been run on the company. I wouldn't know if the work was actually done on these fields—" she pointed to several items "—but these fields here are ghost fields. There are no such numbers."

Zach rubbed his chin. "So, who should've known that these fields were bogus?"

"The field manager, for sure."

"What about someone in accounting?" he asked.

"That depends. If the person issuing the check was new, he or she might not know. But I think the supervisor should've overseen the billing and questioned the charges."

Reaching out, his hand covered hers. He lightly squeezed her hand. It seemed all her senses sprang to life. The feel of his large, rough hand on hers was heavenly. She wanted to reach out and run her fingers up the length of his arm, taste his lips again, feel the strength of his arms around her.

When her eyes met his, she saw he was as affected by their contact as she was.

Slowly, he drew his hand back, his fingers skimming over her knuckles and fingers. She sucked in a breath.

Without breaking eye contact, he whispered, "Thanks for your inside information. It helps, gives me a place to look."

"Anytime, Zach."

And she didn't mean reports.

Zach didn't wake with a start, but he became instantly aware of Toni moaning in her sleep. When his eyes adjusted to the dimness of the room, he saw Toni's head moving back and forth.

"No," she whispered.

She struggled against some unknown demon and opened her mouth. Afraid her cry would wake and frighten the girls, he reached over and placed his hand on her shoulder.

"Toni, Toni, wake up." He lightly shook her.

Her eyes flew open and panic colored them. Before he could stop himself, he rested his palm on the side of her face and forced her gaze to his.

"Toni, you're all right."

Her eyes focused on him, and instantly the fear left them. His hand slid down her neck. The feel of her skin was like that of petals of a rose. When he started to pull his hand away, she rested her hand on his.

He felt her swallow. "Give me a minute, please."

Her body trembled. He moved to her side, pulled her in his arms, letting her rest against his body.

"I'm sorry, Zach," she mumbled against his neck. "I was dreaming of the accident."

"Yours or your dad's?"

"Mine. It's been years since I had that dream." She paused. "It's just as terrible now as it was eleven years ago."

"Do you want to tell me about it?" he asked.

"No. Yes. I don't know." Her hand flexed where it rested on his chest. Suddenly, Zach's thoughts had nothing to do with helping her through this crisis.

"The dream is about Bobby Ray and me as we're driving to the dance."

"Bobby Ray?" he asked, unable to help himself. Since he'd gotten to know Toni, his self-control had taken a major hit.

She smiled, and he felt every damn inch of it. "Yeah. Bobby Ray. His brother was Jimmy Ray, and his sister was Sammy Ray."

Then her lips and her eyes grew dark. "Bobby Ray and I had just started to go with each other. He was the star receiver on the football team. And it was our junior prom. He'd borrow his dad's car, so we wouldn't have to ride in his old pickup. We'd stopped for a red light." She paused, and her struggle was clearly reflected on her face. "When the light turned, we started up. The tanker ran the light and broadsided us. Bobby was instantly killed. It took them—it seemed forever—but I don't know, maybe a half hour to cut me from the wreck. The pain was so searing, that I finally passed out. But I remember seeing what was left of Bobby Ray. I felt guilty for living."

He rested his cheek in her hair. "There was nothing you could've done to prevent what happened."

"I know. But it took me years to realize that."

He felt the warmth of her tears, and it touched him in a way he'd never experienced before. With his thumb, he gently raised her face to his and reverently kissed the tracks of her tears. His body wanted more, but he tucked her head under his chin.

"Go back to sleep, Toni. You're safe."

She snuggled against him, and oddly enough he wanted to make things right for her. If he could keep the demons away, he'd hold her the entire night.

When Toni woke up the next morning, she was alone in the bed. The place where Zach slept was cold.

"Hurry up, Momma," Lisa called as she ran into the bedroom. "Dad's poured the Froot Loops. They get soggy if you wait too long."

Toni's heart skipped a beat. To be called Momma was a dream she always had. She glanced at the little girl. Lisa was dressed in jeans and a T-shirt. Her socks matched and her shoes were tied.

"Did you dress yourself?" Toni asked.

"Kinda. Dad got it out for me, but I put it on. He did help tie my shoes."

"Let me get up, and I'll be there in ten minutes."

As Toni showered, she thought about what Zach had done for her last night. He'd helped drive away the demons that had plagued her. It had been years since she'd had that particular dream. But the years hadn't dimmed its gore. What had driven away the fear was Zach's strong, warm body next to hers.

Minutes later when she entered the kitchen, she smiled as Zach and the girls ate their Froot Loops. He glanced up and asked, "Do you want some?"

"No, I'll just have an English muffin."

After the girls went to their room to get their sweaters, Toni grasped Zach's arm as he walked by.

"Thank you for your help last night. It made a difference, believe it or not."

His hand rested on her neck. "Anytime, Toni. Anytime."

As he walked out of the room, Toni knew she'd already lost her heart.

Zach drove out to the field supervisor's office. He needed to talk to Ollie Townshed. When he asked where the man was, one of the workers offered to call him on his mobile phone.

"Do you know where he is?"

"Sure, he's out at field number three."

"I'll drive out there." Zach pinned the man with a glare. "I'd appreciate if you didn't tell him I'm coming. We're running a security check, and I need to surprise him."

"Sure," the other man agreed.

When Zach drove up to the field, Ollie was walking toward his car.

Zach immediately got out of his car. "Ollie Townshed?"

"Yes. And you're Zachary Knight." He shook Zach's hand. "What are you doing here?"

"I need to ask you some questions."

"Sure. What do you want to know?"

"Remember the incident several weeks ago where we found the gauger's body?"

"Sure."

"When I got back the report on that field, they said that the pump jack hadn't been serviced for quite some time. Now, according to billing records, it had just been looked at.''

''What's that got to do with me? You need to talk to Carl Ormand.'' The hostile quality of his voice told Zach the man had something to hide.

''When I asked Carl about Caprock, he told me that you had highly recommended them. Now, after looking at Caprock's account and how often they've billed us, I wondered if you noticed any problems with their work. Maybe they've billed us for work that they haven't done.''

''I haven't noticed any problems with them.''

''You are the person who originally recommended them to Anderson, aren't you?''

He eyed Zach. ''No, Carl Ormand did.''

''That's what I wanted to know.'' Zach turned to go. As he drove off, Zach wondered how long it would take for Ollie to call his accomplices. And he wondered if one of those accomplices was Carl.

Later that day, as Zach drove home, his mind was filled with the information he'd uncovered so far. As far as the Chamber of Commerce and the city of Midland were concerned, there was no organization named Caprock Service Company. There was no record of the company in the sister city of Odessa, either. No Caprock anywhere. And when he'd questioned Carl, the man had been emphatic that Ollie had recommended the company.

Zach wondered about the suite address that the phantom company used. He wondered what the new engineer would turn up on the other fields that Caprock had serviced. If Ollie was in on the scam, then he'd be useless in helping to expose the fraud. The more he looked into this situation, the worse it became.

The streetlight a hundred yards in front of him changed from yellow to red. Zach's foot pushed down the brake pedal. Nothing happened. The last thing he remembered was his car hitting the stopped car in front of him, then nothing.

"How is he, Doctor?" Toni asked as she stood. The girls, seated on either side of her, reached out and touched her. Toni grasped their little, seeking hands. George, who had met Toni at the hospital after she called, grasped Lori's other hand.

"Your husband is a very fortunate man. He had on his seat belt and the airbag in the car absorbed most of the impact. He's bruised, and has a slight concussion. We'd like to keep him for observation, but he's very insistent that he go home."

Relief flooded Toni. This incident made her realize how much she'd come to care for Zach.

"Is Daddy going to be okay?" Lisa asked, her face filled with worry. Lori, too, watched Toni with anxious eyes.

"Yes, sweetie, he is." Toni turned to the doctor. "The girls' mother was just killed in a car accident, doctor, and I'm sure Zach's thinking about the girls."

"Mr. Knight explained that to me in his own, uh— terms, so I want you to keep careful watch on him during the night. I'll tell you what to watch for. If something happens, call for an ambulance."

"Anything you want."

The doctor nodded and explained the signs that she had to watch for during the night. After he gave her the instructions, Toni was allowed to see Zach. His eyes were closed when she entered the room. His right eye was swollen and beginning to turn black. His right arm was in a sling.

Walking to his side, Toni gently brushed the hair off his forehead. He opened his eyes.

"I hope I don't look as bad as your expression says I do."

Her smile trembled and she swallowed back her tears. "No, you don't look that bad, but I'm afraid you might frighten the girls."

"I could stay away for a few days," he offered.

She lightly touched his cheek. "No. They need to see you and be sure that you're okay. Since they've so recently lost their mother, they're nervous."

He didn't look convinced.

"What happened, Zach?" she asked.

He frowned. "The brakes in my car failed and I rear-ended another car."

"Had you had any problems with them before the accident?"

"It was a new car, Toni. I have a feeling that the brakes didn't fail by themselves."

Her eyes widened as the ugly truth of his statement hit her. "You don't mean that they were deliberately tampered with?"

"It would make sense."

"Why?" Her brow wrinkled. "I mean, who'd want to hurt you?"

"The individual or individuals who are stealing from your dad's firm. Ollie wasn't too cooperative when I talked to him this afternoon."

"Ollie Townshed?"

"Yes. He's the one who recommended Caprock to Carl."

She couldn't imagine Ollie stealing from the company. "I've known Ollie for years. After his wife divorced him, he become distant, but I remember him as a man who laughed at the world."

Zach gaped at her. "Well, the Ollie Townshed I met today didn't have a laugh in him and hadn't for years. He looked like he'd put in some hard years."

"Can we come in?" George asked from the doorway. "I have two little girls who want to see their dad."

Toni nodded, and the door opened to reveal the girls. Lisa rushed in, but Lori followed at a slower pace.

"Hi, guys," Zach murmured. "I'm sorry I was late for dinner, but I had a little accident."

Both of the girls' faces were solemn. After they studied Zach for several minutes, Lisa asked, "Are you going to die, like Momma?"

Zach rested his hand on her head. "No, Lisa, I'm not going anywhere."

Her eyes lit with joy. "Promise?"

"I promise." He turned to Lori. "What about you, Lori? Do you have any questions?"

She looked at his arm in the sling. "Did you break your arm?"

"No, but I hurt it and will have to wear this sling until it gets better."

"Kinda like me," Lori added.

"Just like you."

Lori puffed out her chest and smiled.

Chapter 10

Toni turned on the light on her nightstand. Standing, she walked around the bed and shook Zach.

"Zach, Zach, wake up."

His eyes fluttered opened and he focused on her. The speed at which he did so amazed Toni. "I need to check your eyes." She took the penlight from the nightstand on his side of the bed and flashed it in his eyes. His pupils contracted.

"Good. You're doing fine."

He closed his eyes and turned onto his side. "Then turn off the light and come back to bed."

For an instant, another vision danced through Toni's mind. She hurried around the bed, turned off the light and slipped back into bed.

"Toni," he whispered, his voice dark and seductive.

"What?" Her heart sped up with worry.

"Next time you check my pupils, you might want to put on a robe."

Her jaw fell open and she stared at him in the darkness. Why, he'd been looking. She didn't know whether to be flattered or upset.

But as she turned away from him, her mouth curved into a smile.

So, he'd noticed.

Good.

''Zach, you should at least take the day off,'' Toni said as she helped Zach button his shirt. Toni had complained that he needed to stay at home. But Zach had suffered worse injuries on a mission and finished it without problem. His only concession to the situation was he let her do up the buttons on his shirt.

What he hadn't counted on was the torture of standing this close to her and catching a whiff of her floral perfume. Nor had he counted on the brush of her fingers against his chest as she buttoned the shirt.

Her head was bent and he wanted to lean down and nuzzle her ear, to taste that sensitive skin beneath her ear that he'd caught glimpses of when her hair swayed. During the night, as Toni got up to check on his condition, he'd felt an incredible peace. Something he'd never experienced before. He'd puzzled over the feeling during the early hours of the morning and discovered that feeling was contentment. No one up to this point in his life had ever worried about his personal health. His mother, his ex-wife hadn't given a damn.

''There,'' she whispered and looked up, straight into his eyes.

Everything stopped. Toni's hands contracted on his chest. With the slightest effort, he could bring her flush against his body and cover her lips with his own.

You'd be a fool if you gave in to the urge, he counseled himself. But damn, sometimes he wondered which path was really the foolish one.

Wanting darkened her eyes. Her tongue darted out to wet her lips. It was too much temptation. His arm slid around her waist. His hand splayed wide, bringing her closer to his body.

"Zach, we shouldn't," she whispered, but it was the sweetest denial he'd ever heard.

A smile curved his lips. "You're right," he agreed. "We shouldn't." But that didn't stop him.

Slowly, with great care, his mouth covered hers, sinking into the softness of her mouth, molding the curves of her body into his. He was like a starved man, and she was a banquet for his soul. Her lips moved under his, opening, and welcoming him to deepen the kiss.

His tongue slid into her warmth. She tasted of coffee, woman and want. Her hands grasped his shirt as she gave herself up to the kiss.

He pulled back to trail kisses across her cheek to that place on her neck which he wanted to taste. Her head fell back, giving him access to the sensitive spot.

"We're ready," Lisa called out as she ran into the room.

Zach raised his head, but didn't release Toni.

"Daddy, you're not ready," Lisa scolded.

Oh, but he was. He looked at his daughter. "You're right. I'll have Toni put on my sling, and we'll be out of here."

"Good, 'cause for show and tell, I want to bring Sam, and I need help with his rope."

Both Toni's and Zach's eyes widened.

"Lisa," Zach replied. "We'll have to talk. Wait for me in the living room."

Lisa pursed her lips and stomped out of the room.

Toni's mouth curved into a smile, and she rested her forehead on his chest.

Zach felt as dazed as she did. After what had just happened between them and his child's actions, he felt punch drunk. He released Toni's waist, but his hand captured her chin.

"That shouldn't have happened, Zach," Toni said softly, lowering her eyes so she didn't have to meet his.

"You're right."

Her gaze snapped back to his.

"But it did, Toni. And both of us participated in the kiss."

Her cheeks flamed. "So, what are we going to do about it?" she asked him.

He wasn't ready to take the next step that her questioned implied. He wasn't willing to give in to the passion building up inside him. "Try to ignore it." Of course he didn't mention that it would be like trying to ignore an elephant in your living room—or more aptly, in the bedroom.

"It might be easier, Zach, to stop the sandstorms in the spring, than to ignore this—" she motioned with her hand.

He took a deep, calming breath, trying to fight off the effects of the hunger in his soul. "You're right. But I gave you my word, Toni. This shouldn't have happened. I'm sorry."

Oddly enough, his reassurance and apology didn't seem to soothe her. Rather, she frowned.

"We better go talk to Lisa before she drags Sam to the car." She walked from the room, leaving him to put his injured arm in the sling himself.

* * *

Zach frowned at the mechanic. It was the kind of look that made a grown man gulp. Toni watched in amazement as Zach changed from the man who held her so tenderly this morning into his no-nonsense business mode. The man standing before her now was the type of man whom Toni had been exposed to all her life.

"I understand the car was towed here last night," Zach said, each word ringing with certainty. "What I'm asking you to do is walk back there, get under it and see if the brake line has been cut." There was no room for misunderstanding in Zach's tone. The ugly bruising around Zach's eye only added to the fierceness of his expression.

The mechanic's eyes widened. "Sure, I can look." He walked out into the lot where the wrecked cars were kept. It only took a few seconds for the man to return. "Your suspicion was right. The line had been tampered with."

Zach's expression hardened. "Call the police, and tell Detective Phelps about what you've found."

"I'll do that."

"How long before I can get the car fixed?" Zach asked.

"It will take a couple of days."

Zach nodded and headed out of the building. His jaw was clenched, and fire burned brightly in his eyes. He stopped by Toni's car and took several deep breaths. "I could've had the girls in the car with me," Zach muttered as his fist hit the hood of her car.

She touched his arm and looked into his eyes. "But you didn't, and thankfully you are okay."

"It could happen again, Toni."

His words made her blood run cold. "You don't think that Ollie had anything to do with this, do you?"

"It's damn suspicious that I ask him about Caprock and the next thing I know, my brakes have been cut and I'm rear-ending another car."

"What do you plan to do?" she asked, worried about the steel in Zach's eyes. Whenever her father got that particular look, all hell was fixing to break loose.

"Don't you have a class you have to teach this morning?" he asked her.

Toni glanced down at her watch. He was right. She needed to be at the university at ten. "I do."

"Then why don't you drop me off at work?"

As sure as she knew the sky was blue and Midland was flat, she knew Zach would go searching for Ollie. "Why don't we drive by his office in the oil field and see if he's there?"

Zach's expression hardened. "Why?"

"Maybe Ollie was nervous talking to you. Sometimes your expressions are, uh—formidable. I've known Ollie for a number of years. He might talk to me."

"I don't think that's a good idea."

"So, you think coming down on him like the wrath from above is going to make him cooperate?"

Surprise flickered in his eyes.

"Zach, why don't we see if he's in his office? If he isn't, then I won't bug you about it."

He considered her request, then nodded. "But if he isn't there, I don't want you to pursue it any further."

"You've got a deal."

The detour to the field supervisor's office took less than fifteen minutes. When they walked into the building, Ollie glanced up from his desk. His eyes narrowed.

Before the men could start sparring, Toni smiled. "Good morning, Ollie. It's been a long time since I've seen you."

The older man turned to Toni. "You're looking mighty pretty, Miss Anderson."

"I'm a Mrs. now."

Surprise flickered across the older man's face. "Congratulations. Who's the lucky man?"

"I am," Zach said. The words fell like a lead ball into the quiet.

Ollie nervously looked at Zach. "You look like you've tangled with a buzz saw."

"No. Odd thing happened last night. Seems my brakes were cut, and I ran into another car. That happened right after I talked to you about Caprock."

"So?"

Zach crossed his arms across his chest. "I don't believe in coincidences."

Ollie's jaw hardened.

Toni stepped forward. "Do you know anything that might help us out, Ollie? I mean, Zach could've had his twin girls in the car when the accident happened. And you wouldn't want anything to happen to those precious four-year-old girls, would you?"

Ollie looked from Zach to Toni. "I don't know anything about what happened. Now, I got some fields to see to." He walked out of the building and hopped in his truck.

"He knows something," Zach said, watching the older man race away.

Toni had to agree.

As they drove back to Anderson Oil, Toni recalled the slight limp in Zach's steps. She remembered back to the night Wayne had been killed. Zach had limped then, too.

"Zach, are you all right? Were your legs hurt in the accident and you didn't tell me?"

His eyes narrowed. "Why do you ask?"

"Because you've been limping. It's slight, to be sure. It took me so long after my accident to be able to walk normally that I guess I'm just more in tune to that situation than others." She shrugged.

He sighed. "My limp is an old injury. Whenever I get very tired or my body is stressed, the limp returns."

Unvoiced questions filled her eyes.

He read her thoughts, and she thought he wasn't going to answer her. But finally he said, "On my last mission, we were retrieving some missiles from a terrorist group. As we were leaving with the merchandise, an alarm went off. The folks from whom we took the items objected and shot at us. I took a few bullets in my legs, tearing up the muscles pretty badly. I'm fine now, but my legs wouldn't hold up on a mission, so I left the military."

So he knew about leg injuries. And maybe he identified with Lori.

"Sometime we should compare scars," she suggested teasingly. When she glanced at him, she saw the heat in his eyes.

"I don't think so."

He was right.

"Are you telling me that you think Ollie Townshed skipped town?" Zach asked Martin Phelps, the detective assigned to Wayne Thompson's murder case. After Toni had dropped him off at work, Zach had called the detective earlier in the day and informed him of his interview with Ollie this morning and yesterday afternoon. Zach also included last night's incident with his brakes failing.

"That appears to be the case. When we went to his apartment, the manager said that Ollie stopped by his office and told him he was moving out at the end of the month."

A curse tumbled from Zach's lips. "The man wasn't too forthcoming with me, yesterday. And this morning when my wife and I talked to him, he was less cooperative."

"Did you leave your car unattended after you spoke to Mr. Townshed?"

"I drove it back here to Anderson and talked to Carl Ormand about the situation. He insisted that Ollie recommended Caprock. They pointed the finger at each other."

"I'll say you were lucky that all you got was a black eye and bruised ribs."

"I know that. But I think Ollie is the key to this thing."

"I think you're right. I'll look into Mr. Townshed's background. From where the man lived, he wasn't rolling in dough."

"Maybe Ollie had some expensive habits," Zach offered.

"I'll ask the guys in bunko if they have anything on this guy."

"Thanks, Martin. I've got some things here at the company to look at. It might clue me in to what's happening."

"I got back the autopsy report on the dead gauger," Martin told him. "The coroner in Lubbock wasn't too backed up with bodies. That's why we got the report back so quickly.''

It had been a couple of weeks since they found the dead gauger, and Martin thought that timing was speedy?

Martin laughed. ''I was teasing.''

''What did the M.E. conclude?'' Zach asked.

''He found that the victim was hit from behind with a blunt object. The scene in the field was staged. His injuries weren't consistent with his falling off the stairs of the reserve tank.''

''So, our victim was murdered.''

''Yup.''

''And now we have a missing field engineer and missing records from that field. This stinks more with each new piece of information we get.''

''That it does.'' He paused. ''I'll let you tell your boss. I don't believe I want that job.''

''You're chickening out?'' Zach teased. Martin had been cooperative and informative. Zach liked the detective.

''Nope, I'm just exhibiting wisdom. Your boss has a reputation.'' With those words, he hung up the phone.

Shaking his head, Zach pulled up the file for Caprock on his computer.

When the intercom buzzed, his secretary told him he had a call.

''Zach, this is David Spears. So far I've checked four of those fields that George asked me to look at for you. Half of them were serviced. The other half weren't.''

''Any identifying labels on the equipment?''

''Nope. Do you want me to investigate the rest of them?''

"Yeah, do that. I want to know what I'm dealing with here."

"I'll get back as soon as possible."

Zach hung up. This wasn't going to be easy.

"Are you ready to go home?" Toni asked from the doorway of his office.

He glanced up from the screen. "Yeah, let me print out Caprock's account and take it home with me." As soon as the printer spit out the pages, he shut down his machine.

Toni picked up the business card of the police detective that Zach had called. She raised her brow. "Who is this?"

"The detective assigned to investigate the gauger's death."

"Was he here?" Toni asked.

"Nope. I called him about Ollie earlier in the day. Martin just called back to tell me that it looks like Ollie's skipped town."

Setting down the business card, she sighed. "I don't want to believe he was involved in anything."

"We're looking into his personal finances to see if he has any unusual habits. Also, they confirmed our suspicions. The gauger was murdered."

"How do they know?"

"The coroner says he was hit from behind with a blunt instrument." He further explained what he knew.

She shook her head. "It's still hard to believe."

"Sometimes we have to accept truths we don't like." He should know about that. There were a lot of ugly truths in his own life that he wished he could ignore, but knew he couldn't.

"Let's go get the twins," Toni softly said.

Oddly enough, the thought of his girls brought a

smile to his face. He wondered what Lisa and Lori had done today. He'd hear about it soon enough.

"We need to stop by your dad's office. I've got to update him on what we know."

Toni winced. Zach had to agree.

Zach listened to the giggling coming from the bathroom. It sounded like the twins and Toni were having a wonderful time, and he found himself walking down the hall to investigate.

"Look, I can keep the bubble up in the air," Lori announced. He heard her blow out a breath.

"I can keep it up longer," Lisa answered. An exhaled breath followed.

"Oh, that's good, girls, but I bet I can do it the longest," Toni said.

Curiosity drew Zach. Laughter wasn't something that had filled his life. The sound was so sweet and golden, he wanted to smile in return and join in the fun.

Zach stopped at the doorway and watched as Toni and the girls tried keeping aloft the bubbles from the girls' bubble bath. When one big bubble started to fall, he stepped into the room and blew it upward.

"Good, Daddy," Lisa cried out. "Keep it up."

Toni's startled eyes flew to his. He only caught a glimpse of her before he trained his eyes on the bubble again and tried to keep it from falling.

The girls' giggling and Toni's encouragement surrounded him as he kept the bubble in the air for a long time. When it popped, Lisa sighed.

"Do it again, Daddy," she demanded.

Lori also nodded.

He couldn't resist. He found another bubble and

blew it into the air. As he followed it around the bathroom, the girls offered their encouragement. Finally, the bubble drifted into the hall and burst against the wall.

"Again, Daddy," Lisa cried.

"I think it's time for us to finish our bath and go to bed," Toni answered.

Zach shrugged. "She's right."

"Will you come tomorrow night and do it again?" Lisa asked.

"Please, Daddy," Lori begged. "You're the best one of us."

Pleasure filled Zach. "I sure will."

He walked back into the kitchen and listened as the girls finished bathing. Had he ever played like that in his life? Not in his childhood, that's for certain. And what he did for recreation while in the military, well none of it included bubbles in that innocent role.

"Daddy was really good," Lisa commented. "He kept that bubble in the air a long time."

"Yeah, and he had so much breath," Lori added.

A smile curved his mouth and pride filled his heart. Whoever would've thought a conversation about bubbles would interest him so? But then again, whoever would've thought he'd be playing like that?

His daughters were proud that he could keep a soap bubble aloft. Reason said it was a piddling thing. But his heart didn't accept that assessment of the situation.

Sometimes, he wondered if he pinched himself, would he wake and realize all this had been a dream? He certainly hoped not, because this reality had a certain charm.

* * *

"Daddy, where are you?" Lisa called out from her bedroom, the distress in her voice evident.

The cry wrenched Toni awake. Glancing at the other side of the bed, Toni noted that Zach wasn't there. She hurried into the hall in time to see Zach walk out of the living room. With his uninjured arm, he scooped up Lisa and carried her into her room.

"I was afraid," Lisa mumbled into his neck.

Toni moved to the doorway of the girls' room.

Lisa's fingers moved over Zach's bruised cheek. "Does it hurt?"

"Nope."

She hugged his neck and whispered, "Don't ever go away, please."

His fingers wiped away tears from her cheeks. "I won't. I'm your daddy and I'll always be your daddy, no matter what."

Her mouth turned up in a trembling smile. "'Kay."

He carried her back to bed and settled her under the covers. "Are you ready to go back to sleep?"

She nodded.

He leaned over and brushed a kiss across her forehead. Toni's heart swelled with emotion. The man had reached past her guard and touched her heart with that simple kiss on his daughter's forehead. He turned and saw Toni in the doorway. She stepped out into the hall, trying to still her racing heart. What she was feeling was dangerous, suicidal and definitely not smart in the arrangement she and Zach had made. But as sure as rain in the spring, Toni knew her heart was gone.

When Zach appeared in the hallway, he took her hand and led her into the living room before he spoke.

"I couldn't sleep, so I decided to look over the papers on the Caprock account. That's when I heard Lisa.''

It was obvious to Toni that he was embarrassed to be found comforting his daughter. Unable to stop herself, Toni cupped his cheek. ''When Lisa grows up, she won't remember the fear that woke her, but she'll remember that her father was there when she was frightened. And that will make the difference in her life. She'll also remember a father who can keep a bubble in the air.''

His eyes bore down into hers. ''Was your dad there for you?''

Her thumb brushed over the roughness of his cheek, and she felt the heat from his bare chest under her arms. He only wore a pair of running shorts. ''Not as often as I would've liked, but when he was home, I knew I could count on him.'' Her eyes focused on his well-formed lips and she wanted to taste them again.

Slowly, she rose on tiptoes and pressed her mouth to his. At first, he hesitated, then he moaned and his arms slid around her waist and he pulled her to him. He paused, and she remembered his injured arm.

''Are you all right?'' she asked.

''Maybe that pain was a good thing. I promised not to press you for sex.''

Her trembling fingers stroked his face. ''What if I release you from that promise, Zach?''

His eyes darkened with desire. ''Be sure, Toni, before you make that move, that that's what you want. Because, I know right now, if we walk into that bedroom together, I won't be able to stop until I'm inside you and part of you.''

Her heart nearly exploded with emotion. He was trying to protect her against himself and maybe herself.

In the end, it was the easiest decision of her life. Her peace and assurance must have shown on her face. Grasping his hand, she turned toward the bedroom.

"Wait, let me turn out the lights in living room."

Toni watched as he switched off the lamp. When he joined her in the hall, he took her hand and led her to their bedroom. He closed the door behind them. Leaning back against it, he gathered Toni close. "My arm is going to make things a little awkward, but I think we can probably work around it."

She looked deep into his eyes. "It's your heart, Zach, that's impresses me, not your technique."

His hand came up and framed her face. "Toni, you're killing me with your mouth."

"What?" Before she could get him to clarify himself, his lips covered hers, and all thoughts of explanation fled her brain.

With the softest of touches, he tasted her lips, then urged open her mouth and drank of the essence that was her.

Relief flooded Toni. She wanted to reach out and touch this man, know his body and soul. Toni held nothing back. Her hands rested on his shoulders and her tongue dueled with his, dipping into his mouth to run along the surfaces of his teeth and cheeks.

She felt every wonderful inch of him cushioning her body. His legs were strong and sturdy, his chest like steel, covered with warm living flesh. His was a strength that comforted and drew her.

Through the flimsiness of her nightgown, his skin burned into hers.

His lips trailed down her neck and he lightly bit the sensitive skin at the base of her neck. Her hands contracted on his shoulders.

He smiled down at her, his eyes full of satisfaction. "So you're sensitive there?" he asked darkly.

"Yes." Her hands roamed over his chest, feeling the varying textures, from the smoothness of his skin, to the roughness of the narrow wedge of hair that ran down his stomach to disappear in the waistband of his shorts. Her fingers traveled up to his bruised cheek and eye, lightly skimming over the puffy skin.

"I'm so grateful that you weren't seriously hurt." Her eyes filled with compassion. Lightly, her lips brushed over the area.

He took a deep breath, then lightly kissed her forehead and pulled her to his chest. After a long moment, he said, "I'd like to carry you to bed, but—"

Leaning back, she smiled, took his hand, and led him to the bed. He allowed her to push him down on the bed. She stepped back and pulled her nightgown over her head. Leaning over him, she tugged off his running shorts and briefs.

He pulled her down into his arms. She carefully stretched out beside him, worried that she might hurt his bruised arm. The heat of his body against hers sank into her bones, warming her in a way she'd never felt before. Lightly, her hand roamed over his chest. When her fingers brushed over his nipple, a moan escaped his lips.

She looked up. "Did you like that?"

"Too much." His hand came up and caressed her cheek. "You are so beautiful here." His fingers trailed down her neck to settle between her breasts. "And here," he added, touching the place where her heart rested.

His lips followed the trail his fingers had blazed, and when he took her breast into his mouth, Toni gasped with the pleasure that rolled over her. Her fingers threaded through his hair as she held on, afraid she might disintegrate into a million pieces.

His mouth traveled to her other breast, and he lovingly laved it.

Toni's fingers sifted through his hair, then tugged. When he raised up his head, she covered his mouth with her own. She wanted to give him the joy that he was showering on her.

His hand smoothed down her body, kneading her stomach and hip. When his hand slipped lower, Toni's concentration was centered on the pleasure he gave her.

The tension in her coiled tighter and tighter until she thought she would shatter into a million pieces.

"Zach, please," she whispered.

With ease, he slipped between her legs and entered her. She gasped with the rightness of the joining. Whatever else happened, Toni knew this moment was meant to be.

Wrapping her legs around his hips, she met his thrusts. It only took a moment before she found her release in a shatter of stars and fire. With a final thrust, Zach joined her.

When he caught his breath, he slid to her side and gathered her in his arms.

As she listened to the beat of his heart, Toni knew she'd done the very thing she'd vowed not to do. She'd fallen in love with a man as driven as her father. The thought wasn't comforting.

Zach woke early, before Toni stirred. He still held her in his arms. He was awed by what had happened between them. The sex had been incredible. So incredible, that he wanted to pull Toni under him and wake her with his kisses and loving.

And what was his last thought before he fell asleep last night? Taking Toni again.

Zach sobered. It seemed he couldn't get enough of her. Her smell, the taste of her skin and lips, the smoothness of her cheeks and breasts. He could've happily spent the next month in this bed with her and not felt any urge to go anywhere or do anything but make love to her.

The strength of those emotions frightened him. Hadn't he run this race before and lost? Wasn't his flaming lust for Sylvia evidence that these emotions were temporary? After the sex had died down, they'd had nothing in common.

But Toni's not like Sylvia. She doesn't need you to entertain her, like Sylvia did, his mind argued. Toni didn't moan and complain as Sylvia had done, telling him what a failure he was.

And wasn't Toni wonderful with the girls?

Yes, but what would happen after he won custody of the girls? Would Toni still want to stay with him or would she choose to walk away?

But what worried Zach the most was that the feelings that Toni had ignited in him went deeper and were stronger than anything he'd felt for Sylvia. And that frightened him.

He needed to walk away while he could. So since he couldn't physically leave, he'd put his heart back under lock and key. Because the last time he gave in to his emotions, disaster had struck.

He'd survived last time, but this time, he wasn't so sure he could.

* * *

When Toni woke up, she was alone in the bed. A smile curved her mouth as she thought about the night before. Who would've thought that Zachary Knight was such a tender lover?

She reached out and pulled his pillow to her chest. The essence of the man clung to the case. Wondering where he was, she hurriedly showered, dressed and walked into the kitchen.

He stood staring out the window. From his stance, his arms crossed, a cup of coffee in one hand, Toni knew that things weren't going to go well this morning.

Coldness washed over her. Last night had been a taste of heaven, and she wanted more. Apparently, she had been alone in her wish.

Zach glanced over his shoulder and nodded toward the coffeepot.

"I made coffee."

She pulled a cup from the cabinet and poured herself some of the coffee. When she sipped the hot brew, she was surprised by how good it tasted. "This is good."

He faced her and the corner of his mouth kicked up. "I've watched you. And lucked out."

Leaning back against the countertop, she eyed him. Did she have the nerve to be the first one to bring up last night? She took another sip.

"We didn't use protection last night," he finally murmured.

Her head jerked up. Was that all he was worried about? "That won't be a problem."

"Why is that?"

She didn't want to share this secret right now, but she had no choice. "After the accident and the injuries I suffered, there was so much scar tissue on my fallopian tubes, the doctors told me that I probably could never get pregnant.'' She turned away from him. ''So don't worry.'' Placing her cup on the counter, she went to the pantry. ''I think maybe I'll treat the girls to French toast.''

He came up behind her and turned her to face him. ''I'm sorry, Toni.'' His hands rested on her shoulders. The warmth penetrated her fear.

She swallowed her tears. ''I didn't want you to worry.''

He released her and stepped back. ''I see.''

''I didn't say anything before because I didn't think it would be a problem.''

''You're right.'' He grabbed his cup and took another sip. ''About last night…we can't—''

''I'm hungry,'' Lisa said as she walked into the kitchen.

Surprised, Zach and Toni glanced down at the little girl. As Lisa studied both adults, she nibbled on her bottom lip. ''What's wrong?'' she demanded of Toni, sensing something was wrong. ''Are you going away?'' Panic laced her voice.

''Lisa,'' Lori called out as she limped into the room. Lori's gazed traveled over her sister, then both adults. The child's eyes darkened with worry as she took her sister's hand.

Toni knelt and took both of the girls' hands. ''Nothing is wrong. Your daddy and I were just talking.''

''About what?'' Lisa asked.

Glancing up, Toni hoped Zach would come up with an answer.

''We were talking about the papers I left on the table here. I shouldn't have left a mess for this morning. I'll put them away while Toni makes us French toast.''

Lisa looked back at Toni. ''For sure?''

"For sure."

The child considered the answer, then smiled. "Okay."

Toni breathed a sigh of relief. "Since your daddy can't make the French toast, why doesn't he help you get dressed?"

"But Daddy has a bad arm."

"I know. But he can help you a little. Then by the time you're finished, everything will be ready."

"'Kay."

As Zach ushered the girls out of the room, he glanced at Toni. His expression told her that they still needed to talk.

Somehow, Toni didn't want to finish the conversation that Lisa interrupted. After the joy of last night, she wasn't ready for the bad news Zach had to give her.

Chapter 11

After they dropped the girls off at the preschool, Toni drove toward the dealership where Zach could rent a car.

Zach glanced at Toni. He needed to finish the conversation that Lisa had interrupted this morning. "Toni, we need to finish our talk."

He could see her shoulders tense. "And what is it that you need to say?"

How was he going to put this into words, and not hurt her? "Last night was incredible."

She threw him a surprised glance. "And why does the way you say that make me nervous, like watching a lightning storm over an oil field?"

He sighed. This wasn't going to be easy, but if he didn't stop things now, it would only get worse. "Although the sex last night was unbelievable, I don't think we should cross that line again."

Her hands tightened on the steering wheel. "And why is that, Zach?"

Good question. "Because, Toni, most women, and I think you, too, feel this way, confuse sex with love. And although I'd like to repeat what we did, I think you would associate the act with more than just lust."

"So, you're saying last night was just great sex for you, but nothing else?" A note of disbelief rang through her words.

"I found out the hard way, Toni, that I'm not capable of love."

"You're doing fine with the girls," she countered.

Her point took him off guard. In spite of everything, he felt he'd made progress with Lisa and Lori. "Yes, but that's a different kind of love. Parent-child. And I decided that no matter what, I'd do it for the girls. They're my obligation. I'm not good in the male-female thing. I've already proven that."

"That's a load of horse manure."

Zach's eyes widened. He couldn't quite believe she'd said what she did.

"You can love, Zach. The real question you have to face is, do you want to do it?" She turned into the car dealership and parked the car. Resting her arms on the steering wheel, she turned to him. "When you figure out what you want to do, let me know."

He stared at her, surprised by her reaction.

"I've got a class to teach, Zach."

He took her hint and got out of the car. As he watched her drive away, he realized that her calm response had knocked him for a loop.

She'd pointed out several truths. He just didn't know if he could accept them.

* * *

After class, Beth slapped the airline ticket down on Toni's desk. "Here's your ticket for your flight to Dallas, and there's a car rented in your name. The conference is at SMU. I didn't reserve a room for you, since you said you wanted to stay with your sister while you were there."

Toni's eyes widened as she stared at the ticket. With all that had happened to her this past month, she'd forgotten completely about the conference she was to speak at. "Oh, rats."

Beth rested her hands on her hips. "You forgot?"

Toni glanced at her wall calendar. There, marked with a red pen, was the note on the conference. Looking at the ticket, she noted that the airplane left in less than two hours, just enough time for her to run home, pack and get to the airport.

"Thanks, Beth." Toni grabbed her purse, her speech, and raced to her car. The drive from Odessa, where the university was located, to her house in Midland took less than fifteen minutes. After she packed an overnight bag, she called Zach.

"Zach, I have to speak at a conference in Dallas tomorrow. I'm also booked to do a couple of interviews this afternoon."

"Isn't this sudden?" he asked.

"It's been scheduled for months. I forgot with everything that's happened."

"The girls will wonder what happened to you."

His point tore through her heart. "I'm sorry I didn't mention something to them this morning." She didn't mention that the tenseness between them was what occupied her mind. "You might take the girls to my dad's for the evening. He would certainly entertain them. He's a whiz at playing Old Maid."

A choked sound came through the phone line.

"It might help, Zach. And it would keep the girls busy, and maybe divert them from any worries they might have. I'll try to go by the day school and say goodbye."

"When are you scheduled to return?"

A warm feeling washed through her. "I should be back late tomorrow night. I'll be on the last flight in from Dallas."

"Good luck on your speech, Toni."

"Thank you, Zach." When she hung up, she thought she'd heard a warmth in his voice. It gave her hope.

Toni sat on the top concrete step that led to her sister's backyard. She stared at the large garden planted there. The door opened and J.D. walked out. Her children and their father were at a baseball game.

"When did you become gardener?" Toni said to her sister.

"I'm not. It's Luke."

A startled look crossed Toni's face. "The homicide detective?"

"There's more to the man than looking at the seamy side of life. He grew up a farm boy in the panhandle. His garden is a tribute to that."

Odd, but Toni had never thought of Luke in the way J.D. just described him. For Toni, Luke was the tough detective who had a soft spot for his wife and children. Maybe she should look at Zach in another light. But what?

"What's changed?" J.D. asked.

Startled, Toni glanced at her sister. "What makes you think anything changed?"

J.D. folded her arms across her chest. "Because,

baby sister, I could always read you like a book. And you have a look about you that says you just lost your best friend.''

It was pointless to try to deny anything to J.D. Her sister had always been able to ferret out her secrets. J.D. was the first one who understood the guilt that Toni felt for surviving the accident that killed her date. J.D. also was the person who encouraged Toni to move away from home and try her own wings.

''What's happened between you and Zach?'' J.D. persisted.

Toni's eyes met J.D.'s. ''What makes you think something has happened between us?'' Toni hoped she could bluff her way through this conversation.

''Quit stalling, Toni. What's happened?''

What should she say? ''Things have gotten complicated.''

J.D.'s eyes narrowed. ''You've slept with him, haven't you?''

Toni gaped at her sister.

''I thought so. You have that look about you.''

''And what look is that?'' Toni demanded.

''Lovesick.''

''Well, if I remember correctly, you didn't intend to marry Luke, but did. And I have the sneaky suspicion you found yourself in the same position that I'm in.''

''You're right.'' J.D. looked out into the yard.

''So, how did you and Luke work it out?'' Toni asked.

''When you come close to death, which we did on the case we were working on, it puts things into perspective. As a technique to solve problems, I wouldn't recommend it. But, Toni, you need to decide what's important and what you can live with. Then go after it.''

"The problem is, J.D., I don't know what that is."

"Then, sis, you're in big trouble."

That she did know.

Zach stretched out in the bed, missing the woman who usually slept on the other side. It was stupid, of course, but it was the truth.

Damn, he was in trouble.

The girls had missed Toni at dinner, but George distracted them enough to make them laugh. The card game afterward was quite a revelation. George played a mean game of Old Maid, but oddly enough, Zach's quiet child, Lori, won most of the games.

As the girls got ready for bed, it was obvious that they missed Toni. She'd been the glue that had held them together. Even Sam seemed to miss her.

Zach rolled onto his side. The visions of making love to Toni last night crowded into his brain. Her smell, the taste of her lips, the smoothness of her skin, the exquisite pleasure that their lovemaking brought.

He clamped down on the wild thoughts. What he needed to do was think about the problems at Anderson and think about how Ollie and Carl fit into the picture, not how much he missed Toni.

His last thought as he drifted into sleep was that he was glad Toni would be back tomorrow.

Ollie stared at the man. "They're going to discover what we've been doing. I think we should cut our losses and run."

"You're being stupid. No one can pin anything on you or me."

"Zachary Knight looked mighty angry when he came to the field. If he'd been alone, I don't want to think what would've happened, him being ex-Special Forces."

"He wouldn't have harmed you."

"Easy for you to say. It ain't your butt hanging out. I want out," Ollie demanded.

"You should've done a better job sabotaging his brakes."

Ollie shrugged. "I want my share of the money."

"Fine. I'll meet you out on the public road by the storage tank near field number three. I'll have your money."

As Ollie drove away, the other man decided it was time to take Ollie out of the picture.

He watched as Ollie drove up and parked beside him. He fingered the gun on the seat beside him. He hated that everyone was turning chicken on him. Damn them anyway.

Ollie leaped out of his car. "You got my money?"

The man raised the gun.

"Hey, what do you think you're doing?" Ollie backed away, fear in his eyes.

"I'm making sure that you don't rat on me. Besides, I don't want to share the money." He pulled the trigger and placed a shot between Ollie's eyes. Ollie collapsed like a rag doll.

Calmly, the man got out of his car, retrieved Ollie's keys, and put the body in the trunk.

He thought about running the car into the sludge pit, but he heard the sound of a diesel engine and knew others would soon be here.

With a final look around the area, he was satisfied

that he hadn't left any evidence to connect him with the murder.

He thought about the journals Ollie had, but he didn't worry about them. Those journals would only incriminate Ollie.

Nothing pointed to him.

Zach studied the computer printouts on Caprock. When he'd checked with the accounting supervisor yesterday, she'd also been concerned by the billings. Yes, indeed, what had been paid out to Caprock seemed a bit high, she'd agreed, but this time last year, there had been many cost overruns.

"Zach," his secretary's voice came over the intercom. "Detective Phelps is on the phone."

Zach picked up the receiver. "Afternoon, Detective. What can I do for you?"

"We found Ollie Townshed. His body was discovered in the trunk of his car. He had a bullet through his skull."

Rubbing his neck, Zach sighed. "So, now two of Anderson's employees have been killed. Do you believe in coincidence?"

"No. I think you've got a murderer there."

Zach rubbed his hand over his face. "Do you have any witnesses to Ollie's murder?"

"None. We found the car on the public road near your field number three. The officer who came across it called it in, and discovered Ollie was wanted for questioning. Further investigation led to the discovery of the body. I'm going to go back to his apartment. I'll be able to search it now. Maybe the man left something that would identify his killer."

"I'll bet money is what drove this murder," Zach

commented. "It's been claimed that Ollie recommended a company named Caprock Service to keep up some fields. A substantial sum of money was paid to them."

"When we search his apartment, I'll keep my eye out for anything that might clue us into what Ollie was doing."

"Do you mind if I join you in the search? I won't interfere, but I might spot something that might tell us about Ollie."

After a moment, Martin said, "Sure. Why don't you meet me at Ollie's in about ten minutes?" Martin gave him the address of the unit.

"I'll see you there." Zach was glad he'd rented a car yesterday. He checked his watch. It was a little after one in the afternoon. He had several hours before he had to pick up the girls at day care.

As Zach walked out of the building, he saw Carl talking to a woman in the parking lot. The woman seemed upset from her body language and waving arms. Just as Zach was about to walk over to the couple, the woman turned and walked into the building. She motioned for Carl to follow her. The woman seemed familiar, but Zach couldn't get a clear view of her face.

But Zach somehow had a bad feeling about what he'd just witnessed.

"They're on to us," Stephanie Norman snapped.

"No, they're not," Carl replied.

"That's not what Ollie said to me this morning. Apparently Zachary Knight and his wife have been questioning him about Caprock and the billings for that account."

Carl's nerves were on edge. He didn't need this confrontation here in the parking lot. Had the woman lost her marbles to talk to him out here, where everyone could see them? He looked around and caught a glimpse of Zach as he walked to his car.

"Why don't we discuss this in a more private place?" He stepped closer. "If you aren't careful, you'll be the one to tip our hand. Is that what you want, Stephanie?"

Her eyes darkened with hurt. "No."

"Then why don't you go back to your office and pretend everything is fine. I'll contact you later tonight."

In her eyes, Carl read her panic. He smiled through his irritation. He needed to keep the stupid woman happy for a few more days. Then he could be rid of her.

He gave her a smile, then turned to go. As he walked away, he wanted to scream about the incompetence of some people.

But then again, he'd already disposed of two loose ends. Pretty soon, he could walk away with all the money and no worries.

As he drove to Ollie's apartment, Zach wondered about that scene he had just witnessed. Why was Carl meeting this woman in the parking lot?

When he got to the apartment complex, the police were combing through Ollie's residence. Zach walked around the apartment for a few minutes and then decided to look through the pile of papers on the coffee table. Near the bottom were several bank statements. Glancing at each one, Zach noted that thousands of dollars were going through the man's account.

"Zach," Martin called from the bedroom. "I think we've found something."

He hurried into the bedroom and stopped when he spotted the bound journal on the bed. It was the same kind of journal that they kept out in the fields to note the amount of crude in each storage tank. As he walked forward, Zach saw the name on the spine of the book—Anderson Oil.

Zach looked at Martin. "Is that the missing logbook from field number one?"

"It is, the very one we've been looking for since the murder of Wayne Thompson."

Picking up the book, Zach examined the entries. Although he hadn't worked in the oil industry for long, he knew that this book could prove that someone had been stealing oil. He looked at Phelps.

"We need to compare these figures with official records."

"Detective Phelps, I found some more items." The officer set two boxes on the bed. In the first one was stationery for Caprock, along with envelopes and business cards.

"Everything needed to step up a dummy corporation," Zach said looking at the articles.

In the second box were bank statements for Ollie's checking and savings account, going back several years.

"I wonder," Zach began, "if we can make a connection between the balance in Ollie's account and paid bills to Caprock?"

"We can sure try. Do you have a copy of what Anderson paid to Caprock?"

"I do. Why don't we go back to my house and look through the files?"

"Your house?" Phelps asked.

"I'd rather no one at Anderson sees us. I'm sure someone within the company is orchestrating these thefts and I don't want to tip them off. I have a copy of Caprock's billing for the last year at the house. Since the death of Wayne Thompson, I've been going over Caprock's bills trying to come up with a pattern."

"Okay."

"Besides, my wife used to work in the accounting department of Anderson, and she might see something that you and I might miss. She's flying back into town tonight."

"Your wife?" Phelps asked.

"Antonia Anderson Knight."

Martin's eyes widened. "The daughter of George Anderson?"

"Yes."

"When did this happen? There was nothing in the papers."

Zach shook his head. "Apparently, you don't read the society column or go to First Baptist, do you, Detective? Because I assure you that everyone there knows of my marriage."

Martin shook his head. "Yeah, maybe I should go to church."

When the two men drove up to the house, there were two cars parked in the driveway.

"Seems you have company, Zach," Phelps noted as he walked by Zach's side. The girls bounced out of Zach's car.

"Mom's home," Lisa shrieked, running to the house.

Zach shook his head. "I don't know who that other

car belongs to.'' The cream-colored sedan was nothing fancy, and looked like a government-issued vehicle.

When Zach opened the front door, Lisa charged into the living room.

''Momma, are you here?'' she cried. Lori followed as fast as her cast allowed her to move.

Toni hugged both girls. ''How are you?'' she asked.

''We missed you,'' Lisa answered. ''But we ate with Grandpa last night. And played Old Maid. But you know what? Lori won most of the games.''

Toni smiled at Lori. ''Did you whip Grandpa?''

Her smile sparkled. ''I did.''

Toni laughed. The sound warmed Zach more than he wanted. When Toni glanced at him, he thought he saw joy in her eyes.

''You're early,'' he said stupidly.

Toni's eyes sparkled. ''I caught an earlier flight.''

Someone cleared his throat. Toni stood.

''Zach, I'm glad your home. We have company from the city,'' Toni said, indicating the woman. Toni peaked around Zach and looked at Detective Phelps.

''We've got several city employees here, then,'' Zach began. He turned and said, ''Detective Phelps, I want you to meet my wife, Toni and—''

The other woman stepped up. ''Francis Getty. I'm a social worker with the city. I've come on a surprise visit to check on how you are getting along with your daughters. We wanted to investigate your sister-in-law's claim against you.''

''My ex-sister-in-law,'' Zach corrected.

She nodded her acceptance of the correction. She turned to Detective Phelps. ''Are you with the city?''

''Yes, I am.''

Her gaze turned to Zach. "May I ask why you have a Midland Police detective accompanying you home?"

Zach wanted to shift into his don't-mess-with-me persona that he used while in the service, but when he glanced at Toni, he read the warning in her eyes to cooperate.

"The detective accompanied me home so we could go over some evidence in a murder case. The victim was an employee of Anderson Oil."

Francis turned to Phelps. "Is that so?"

Zach worked hard to cap his anger.

"Indeed it is, Ms. Getty. We came here because Mrs. Knight worked for her father in the accounting department and we wanted her advice on the records."

"I see. Well, I would like to conduct some interviews with Mr. Knight, but we can postpone them until next week." She pulled a business card from her purse. "Please call tomorrow and set up an appointment. We need to get this interview done so the court will have the information it needs."

"Daddy," Lisa asked. "Is somethin' wrong?"

Squatting down, Zach smiled at her. "Nothing's wrong. This lady here wants to see how well you're doing now."

Lisa glanced up. "I like my new house. I've got a daddy, momma, grandpa, lots o' cousins. And a dog. Go away."

Zach pulled his daughter close. When he stood, he still held Lisa.

"Could I interview the children?" Ms. Getty asked.

Zach started to object, but Toni smiled and turned to the woman.

"Since we don't have anything here for dinner, why

don't you talk to the girls while Zach picks us up something to eat?''

Ms. Getty nodded and took the girls into the living room. Zach, Toni and Martin walked into the kitchen. "Is everything okay?" Martin asked.

She glanced at Phelps. "You tell me."

"We have some papers we'd like you to look at," Zach explained.

Her eyebrow arched. "Oh?"

"We found the logbook for the field where Wayne Thomas died."

"Where?" Surprise colored her voice.

"In Ollie Townshed's apartment." Zach saw the wariness in her face. He slid his arm around her shoulders and pulled her to his chest. He whispered, "They found Ollie's body today. He'd been shot."

Toni jerked back and stared at Zach. "Oh, no."

Zach nodded toward the living room. "What are we going to do about that?"

"Don't worry. If Lori could beat my dad at Old Maid, she'll hold her own with the social worker. Why don't you let me order a pizza, then you go and get it? And I think we might include our first guest," Toni added, looking at the detective.

"I'd appreciate a meal."

"Good."

After the girls had been settled in their beds, Toni, Zach and Martin Phelps gathered in the study.

Zach placed the logbook on the desk, then showed Toni the bank statements they had. "We found this stuff in Ollie's apartment. I was wondering if you could tap into the company's computer and check this book against what's recorded for the field."

"Sure."

She accessed the company's computer and, using Zach's security code, she brought up the file. As they studied the entries, the discrepancies became obvious.

"It's not flagrant, so it wouldn't stand out, but it's there. The actual barrels versus what they put down for official count," Toni commented.

"Whoever was doing the stealing was smart. A little here and there, but nothing big to alert people to the scam."

Zach sat back. "Why don't you bring up Caprock's account?"

As they reviewed the entries, Zach pulled out the report the independent engineer had given him. They compared the two.

"It looks like Caprock did some work, but other times, they didn't service the fields they claimed. Also, look here." Toni pointed to two entries. "And here are those phantom fields."

Zach's eyes narrowed. "Why didn't someone in accounting catch these phony charges?"

Martin nodded. "My question, too."

"Maybe the person who did the billing knew they were bogus," Toni answered.

Martin pulled out Ollie's bank statements. "Why don't we compare some of the deposits Ollie made to some of these phony billings?"

It quickly became obvious that each one of the phony charges showed up in Ollie's checking account.

"What about these other deposits?" Martin asked. "There are enough there to worry about."

Toni studied the figures. "Let me think about it. Let me check exactly what Ollie's salary was and we can eliminate those entries.'' It only took a few minutes for Toni to assess his salary.

Over a six-month time period, Ollie had twenty-thousand dollars in deposits, which they were unable to track to a source.

Martin glanced at his watch. It was well after midnight. ''I'd best get home. We can work on this tomorrow.''

Zach walked out with Martin.

''You married a sharp lady, Zach.''

Pride flooded Zach. Yes, indeed, Toni was amazing. ''Thanks. Tomorrow, I'm going to have to tell George Anderson what we've uncovered here tonight—the newest tidbit of bad news.''

Shaking his head, Martin said, ''I don't envy you.''

Zach wasn't looking forward to the prospect, either. Damn, as the head of security, it seemed he was a washout.

When he went back into the study, he turned off the light and slowly walked down the hall. Pausing at the girls' room, his mind went back over the unexpected visit from the social worker. It had only been another blow in a long, long day, which began with the girls' sad faces this morning without Toni there with them, then Ollie's murder, to the surprises they discovered tonight.

What he needed was a good night's sleep.

As he entered the bedroom, Toni finished tying the sash on her robe. The bed had been turned down.

''How did the interview go with the girls and the woman from social services after we left?'' Zach asked, as he unbuttoned his shirt.

Looking up, she pinned him with a gaze. ''Good. The girls weren't shy about talking. And I'm sure the social worker wanted to see if our marriage was a sham or if it was the real thing.''

He slipped off his shirt and sat down on the bed. "So, what do you think she discovered?"

Her face lit with humor. "I think Ms. Getty was a little shaken up when she found me home alone. When I told her you were bringing the girls home, she seemed a bit taken aback.'' Toni laughed. It was full and soft and entirely feminine. And it hit Zach square in the gut, reminding him that he wanted this woman. "She was impressed."

"How'd the time go with her and the girls?" He was nervous about that interview.

"Ms. Getty was surprised by the stories the girls had about how they've helped me in the aviary in the backyard. They wanted her to go look at the bird with a broken wing that we'd been nursing.

"You'd be so pleased with how animated Lori was. Why, when she bubbled up with information on what we'd done, my jaw dropped open.'' Toni sat down on the bed next to him. "You wouldn't have believed it, Zach. That little girl came to life, and her eyes twinkled. It was truly amazing."

Zach didn't know if he was more shocked by the news about his daughter, or the way his body reacted to Toni's nearness. "I wish I could've seen it."

"Oh, Zach, it was such a wonderful thing to see Lori come to life like that. Of course, Lisa didn't take a back seat to her sister, so she told Ms. Getty about how much fun it's been to have Sam and go to Las Vegas and see us get married. Then she went into all the new cousins and uncles and aunts she now had. She was one happy camper."

"And how did Ms. Getty react to that?"

"She was hard to read, but she took a lot of notes. She questioned the girls about you and they said, 'He wasn't too good to start, but he's okay now.' I believe your burial of the goldfish won them over."

He shook his head. "And all this time I thought I had to do something wonderful. Burying a goldfish was all it took."

Her fingers touched his jaw. "It's never the big things, Zach. It's the everyday caring. Helping Lisa wear the right panties on the right day. And making breakfast, and being there when the goldfish die."

His hand covered hers. The desire to believe her washed over him. "You're tempting me to think it was me who made the difference."

"It was, Zach. The girls needed stability in their lives, and you provided it."

A deep hurt in his soul eased. Maybe things would work out. He took her hand and kissed the palm. His eyes locked with hers. The desire coursing through his body was reflected in her eyes.

He lowered his head. Her eyes fluttered closed and a deep sigh echoed in the silence. His lips lightly brushed over hers.

Don't do it. The warnings echoed through his head. *It's a mistake to give in to the passion.*

Just as he started to pull away, her fingers stroked over his cheek and her lips found his again. It was the sweetest temptation he'd ever encountered and he couldn't turn away. His arms wrapped around her and he stretched out on the bed, carrying her down on top of him.

He'd missed her. And wanted her.

Toni's hair curtained them in their own world where

there was nothing but the two of them. His hand stroked down her back, pressing her into his arousal.

"I want you, Toni," he admitted. No matter how much he didn't want these feelings or how much they frightened him witless, they wouldn't go away.

Her eyes met his, her hands framed his face. "It's the same for me, Zach. I missed you last night when I was in Dallas." Her fingers caressed the healing bruises on his face.

Her admission eased his heart. At least he wasn't the only one at the mercy of this attraction.

Toni's lips nibbled down his neck, while her hands skimmed over the skin of his shoulders and chest. As her mouth moved down his chest, her fingers worked on the belt and zipper of his pants. He grasped her hands and pulled her up against him.

His fingers untied the belt of her robe and quickly peeled it off her body. Her nightgown followed. He pulled her down to him, then eased her onto her back. His hand stroked her. He found the scars on her abdomen, and his fingers paused. His gaze found hers. "I'm sorry," he murmured, then lightly kissed a scar.

He heard her gasp, then her hand tangled in his hair and held him close. After a moment, when her grip eased, Zach kissed his way down to her legs. The scars that crisscrossed her legs called out to him. He lovingly kissed each one. When he finished, he glanced up. Toni's eyes sparkled with a deep emotion. One he was afraid to name.

"Come here," she huskily whispered.

A sweeter invitation he'd never heard.

He moved up her body and fitted himself to her. He was home. The thought flashed through his brain.

But the passion that quickly followed didn't leave time for him to think, only to act.

As he stroked her, he heard Toni's breath speed up. Her fingers speared his hair as she moved with him, meeting his thrusts. Together they climbed the mountains until they reached the top at the same time. Her cry of delight was echoed in his.

Afterward, he rested his forehead on hers. When he opened his eyes, Toni met his gaze. She didn't say anything, but he could read her reaction. It was love.

Rolling to his side, he pulled her close, then pulled the sheet over them. He'd just proven to himself that he couldn't stay away from her. And apparently, he wasn't the only one who felt that way. The question was, when would this passion and heat burn out?

She snuggled against him. Picking up his hand, she looked at the scar on the back of it. "How did you get this? Was it from your time in the military?"

"Nope. When I was a teenager, I got into an argument with my mother. She didn't like what I said, so she took a knife and went after me."

Toni blanched. "I'm sorry, Zach."

"Don't worry about it. It was a long time ago."

Her body was tense and Zach felt a tear hit his chest. Damn, he shouldn't have told her. After their intimacy, he should've known not to have shared that ugliness. He'd tried to share with Sylvia, and that had turned into a disaster. He never tried again with another woman. Keep your mouth shut, and then the woman would never have any ammunition. Or pity.

Finally, after a long silence, she asked, "What's wrong, Zach?"

Startled, he looked down. "What makes you think something is wrong?"

"It's a feeling I have. Our loving was wonderful, but I sense that worries you. Why?"

He laughed. A genuine, honest-to-goodness laugh. "I guess you've got me pegged."

"And you're not used to people being able to read you, is that it?"

"I used to have a name in the unit I led. I was called Iron Mask, because no one could ever read me."

She rose up on an elbow. "It's not so hard."

"Now, you're the one trying to put one over on me."

Her expression turned serious. "No. Oddly enough, I'm not. For me, I can sense—"

"What?"

She looked down at his chest. "It's kind of difficult to explain. All I know is I feel connected to you."

Her admission stunned him. His fingers grasped her chin and he brought it up so he could see her face. "I've proven, Toni, that I'm not capable of love. My mother didn't love me." He remembered the accusations that she'd bitterly thrown at him...the names... the anger. "Sylvia, my ex, didn't either. I've accepted that about myself. You don't have to sugarcoat this great sex with sweet words."

Toni's eyes filled with distress. "Zach, there is nothing wrong with you. We all deserve love, and from what I know about you, you've done nothing to merit not being loved. Your mother and Sylvia are the ones who had the problem. Not you."

His hand cupped the side of her head and gently placed it back on his shoulder.

"Believe what you want, Toni," he murmured into the darkness.

"What I believe, Zach, is that you deserve to be

loved.'' The note of conviction in her voice rang through the room.

He smiled, wishing that her words were true.

Toni listened to the beating of Zach's heart while his heat surrounded her. She relived their lovemaking. When Zach had kissed the scar on her abdomen, she'd nearly wept with joy, gratitude and love. When he continued down her legs, touching each scar, laving them with his kisses as if he could absorb those long-ago injuries, his actions had pierced deeply into her heart. No one but her family had ever guessed the hidden pain that she held within herself. Pain for the loss of her friend, pain for the loss of her ability to have children.

But somehow Zach had guessed. His loving attention to those old scars helped her, eased the wounds.

Now, what tore her heart was his belief that he didn't deserve to be loved. What must his mother and ex-wife have done to him? Zach's soul was in the dark, and Toni wanted to pull him into the light. But how?

She'd matched wits with her father, who was as stubborn and hardheaded as Zach, and won. What would it take this time to win against Zach's will?

She didn't know, but she was going to try to find a way to reach him. She wasn't her daddy's daughter for nothing.

Chapter 12

A muscle throbbed in George Anderson's jaw and his eyes hardened when Zach told him the news of how much money had been swindled from the company.

Wariness crept up Zach's spine. "Toni thinks, and I agree," he added, "that maybe we've uncovered the tip of the iceberg."

George stood and walked to the windows of his top floor office. Zach could easily understand how George had become a powerful oilman. The man had a poker face that made Zach nervous.

"Do you think you could've caught this earlier, Zach?" George asked.

That was the question that had plagued Zach for the past couple of days. Could he have caught this stealing any earlier? "I don't know. Although I'm head of security, my main focus is to guard against outside thefts. Not inside jobs."

George turned and looked at him. "Then I guess we'll have to amend your job description."

Amazement raced through Zach. "You're not angry at this situation?"

"I'm plenty mad. And whenever we catch whoever is stealing from me, the bastard better hope the cops get to him before I do. Because if they don't, there won't be any guarantee he'll live long enough to go to trial. I didn't work my fingers to the bone to be ripped off."

Ah, there was the man Zach knew and understood.

"You say that it was my Toni who helped you locate some of the fraudulent billings."

"She was invaluable to me and Detective Phelps."

Pride shone in the old man's face. "She's a mighty smart little lady, which I assume you've discovered yourself."

George Anderson had committed many sins in his life. But the man loved his children and was proud of them. For that alone Zach admired him. That validation had not been given to Zach in his life, and he knew the cost a child paid.

"You're right, sir, Toni is a bright woman." Beautiful and warm, and infinitely appealing. His eyes focused on George, and from his look, Zach must've revealed his heart, because George smiled.

"I've got a piece of advice for you, Zach. Give in. You're only going to prolong your own misery."

Zach knew exactly what George was talking about. Acknowledge his feelings for Toni. That was a step he couldn't even consider at this point, let alone act on.

"I'm going to try to discover if there is anything else to their fraud or if Caprock was the only company they used to steal from Anderson."

George shook his head. "I can't believe Ollie did that to me. He and I go way back. He married his wife the same year I married my first wife. He gave me hell when I divorced J.D.'s mother and married Toni's mom." The old man shrugged. "I was an ass. But that's neither here or there. Several years later, Ollie's wife left him. He took it hard. Started drinking. I tried to help and thought I'd gotten him on the straight and narrow. It appears I didn't."

Listening to George recount his own marriages and Ollie's killed any hope that had sprung to life in Zach's heart that maybe, just maybe, there was such a thing as love.

George shook off the morose thoughts. "Let me know what you turn up."

Zach nodded and left the office. He walked down to the accounting department. He had discussed with Toni this morning the way to go about checking on the billing of the Caprock account.

The head of the department, June Davis, told Zach who was responsible for the account and took him to the woman's desk. Stephanie Norman was a plain woman, with blond hair and a lovely smile. A warning bell went off in Zach's head. He felt as if he'd met Stephanie before, but he knew he hadn't.

"So, you're the only individual who bills Caprock?" Zach asked, trying very hard to appear nonthreatening. He didn't want the woman to clam up.

"Yes."

"Has anyone worked on the account maybe, say, when you're busy or sick?"

"I don't believe she's missed any days this past year," June answered before Stephanie could. "Have you, dear?"

"No."

"There are several bills in their file for phantom fields," Zach stated, wanting to see Stephanie's reaction.

"How do you know that?" June Davis demanded.

Zach gave the woman a cool stare. "I am the head of security for this company, Mrs. Davis. I can access all the accounts on my computer."

She didn't look pleased. "I suppose." She turned to Stephanie. "Please pull up the Caprock account."

It only took a minute for the information to appear on the terminal screen. Mrs. Davis looked over the entries, then frowned. "Stephanie, what is this? There are no such fields as Blue number three and Green number seven."

The woman glanced at her supervisor. "I only pay the bills, Mrs. Davis. I guess I didn't pay attention to all the information on the invoices."

Folding her arms over her breasts, Mrs. Davis frowned. "This is sloppy work, Stephanie. I guess we'll have to audit Caprock. We can have the information to you first thing tomorrow morning."

From the look in Stephanie's eyes, Zach wondered if the promise would be kept. Or if Stephanie Norman didn't want anyone looking too closely at her work.

As he turned to go, Zach noticed a paid bill on the desk. What fascinated him about it was the address. It was the same as Caprock's. He glanced at Stephanie. When she met his eyes, her gaze quickly shifted away.

As Zach hurried back to his office, he heard Toni in the hall. As he turned the corner he found his wife, who was holding Lisa, and glaring at Carl Ormand.

"You ever speak to my girls like that again, Carl,

I'll personally make sure my father cans you within the hour. Do you understand me?''

Carl tried to smile, but it fell flat. And it certainly didn't influence Toni. "I'm sorry," he said. "It was a college squash trophy." When Toni didn't appear impressed, he added, "I guess when one isn't around kids, they lose touch."

"No, Carl. That's not the problem at all." Toni turned and stopped when she noticed Zach.

"Is there a problem here?" Zach asked.

Lisa held out her arms to her dad, and Zach took the child from Toni's arms.

"No, there isn't." Toni didn't glance at Carl, but simply walked toward Zach's office.

Lisa put her head on Zach's shoulder, and rested against him. With a final piercing glance at Carl, Zach followed Toni into his office. Lori sat next to his secretary, chatting about the bird she'd helped Toni with a few days past.

Lori looked up. "Hi, Dad. We just came from the doctor. My cast can come off in—" She frowned.

"One week," Toni said.

"Yeah, one week. I can't wait. The doctor says my skin will be all wrinkly and white. But that's 'kay."

So that was the reason they'd stopped by. "That's wonderful. Would you girls like some popcorn like you had the last time you were here?" Zach asked.

"Yes," the girls chimed.

Looking at his secretary, Zach asked, "Would you please take the girls to the break room, Nancy? I need to talk to my wife for a minute."

"Sure."

Once they were alone in his office, Toni let out a

growl. ''Carl is such a pig. I would've loved to have kicked him in the—''

Zach drew her into his arms and silenced her with a kiss. Toni resisted only for an instant, then melted into his embrace, eagerly returning his kiss.

It had been only a few hours since they had made love, but for him it seemed like a million years as the hunger in him exploded.

His need for Toni was increasing instead of playing itself out. When he heard her voice in the hallway several minutes ago and heard her defending Lisa, his heart had skipped a beat.

She had been defending his children as fiercely as if they were her own. That knowledge was a treasure, one he never thought he would uncover.

He pulled back and rested his forehead against hers. ''We'd better stop while we can. We don't want to shock the children or my secretary.''

Toni laughed. ''Believe me, Nancy has seen a lot. She won't be shocked.''

''So, I assume you came by to tell me about Lori's leg.''

Her smile warmed him deep inside. ''You'd be pleased, Zach. The girls didn't want to wait until tonight to tell you the good news.'' Her fingers lightly skimmed over the healing bruises on his cheek and eye. ''They were positive that you'd want to hear as soon as possible, and that we shouldn't wait.''

Toni's eyes filled with tears. One rolled down her cheek.

''Why are you crying?'' he asked, puzzled by her reactions.

Her bottom lip trembled as she looked into his eyes. ''Because, Zachary Knight, you've won a major battle.

Your little girls are sure enough of your heart to believe you'd want to hear right away that Lori's cast would come off soon.'' Her fingers skimmed across his lips. "Do you understand, Zach? They believe and trust you. It's a gift beyond price.''

Zach pulled Toni to his chest and took a deep breath. She was right. They had reached a milestone and he was awed by his feelings.

Toni pulled back. "Did you bring me in here simply to kiss me or was there another reason?''

He laughed at himself. Toni had an amazing ability to redirect him. No one else had had that ability up until this moment.

"Toni, I just interviewed the woman who oversees the Caprock account. She claimed she didn't pay attention to which fields the bills were for. Her supervisor wasn't happy.''

Toni's brow shot up. "Oh, I don't doubt that. June Davis is very 'particular' about knowing one's accounts. She chewed me out when I couldn't supply from memory a detail on a fitting supply company that I billed.''

Her response further convinced Zach that Stephanie knew what was going on. "When I looked at Stephanie's desk, I noticed a bill from the Plains Drilling Company. But it had the same address, street number and suite number as Caprock.''

Toni's eyes widened.

"Tell me, can you go in and see if there are any other companies with that same mailing address?''

"Sure I can. You want me to go and ask June to do that search?''

Zach shook his head. "No. I want to do that tonight when we get home and compare it with the other deposits in Ollie's account. We don't know who is or isn't involved in this mess."

Toni smiled. "Zachary Knight, I think you may have discovered the scheme."

"I hope." He reached out and pulled her into his arms. Before he could stop himself, his lips settled over hers. Toni welcomed his kiss, opening her mouth and sliding her arms around his waist.

"Daddy, look," Lisa said, rushing into the room. She stopped and stared at Zach and Toni. "Are you doing *that* again?" She crossed her arms over her chest, and the bag of popcorn tipped, spilling the popped kernels onto the floor.

Toni smiled up at him. "I guess we've been caught."

"Next time, I'll be sure to close the door," Zach whispered back.

As they walked out of Zach's office, George called to them.

"Toni, dear, did Zach tell you about the reception tonight at the club?" George asked, stopping before the gathered family.

"What reception?" Toni asked.

Zach blushed. It was so unexpected that Toni could only stare at him.

George rubbed his chin. "So, you didn't tell my daughter about the little shindig I arranged, did you, Zach?"

"With all that's going on, I forgot," Zach admitted.

Toni wasn't surprised by her father's actions. She'd been through enough with him to be able to roll with his punches. "What time, Dad? And what about the girls?"

"Eight-thirty. And I want you to bring the girls. I

want everyone to see my beautiful new granddaughters."

"We won't be able to stay long, Dad," Toni warned. "It will be close to their bedtime."

"Don't worry. This is just an informal get-together. I've planned something fancier next month."

"Talk to me about it first, Dad." Toni left no room for argument with her tone.

"I will."

When George walked off, Toni shook her head.

"Are you upset?" Zach softly asked.

She turned to him and smiled. "Zach, if I got upset every time my dad did something like this, I'd be a miserable human being. But next time, have him deal with me. I may take this in stride, but Dad knows he'll only get one chance to sucker me. Next time, it won't be easy."

Around five that night, Toni, Zach and Martin Phelps gathered in Toni's study again and Toni tapped into the company's computer.

"The company has a database of all its accounts, so if I ask for an account with Caprock's address, it should spit it out for us," Toni explained.

With a few keystrokes, Toni typed the information and hit Enter. Within seconds, a list of three companies appeared on the screen. When she compared the bills of those accounts to the deposits in Ollie's account, most of the remaining items matched.

"Well, I'll be," Martin breathed.

"Let me try something else," Toni said. She altered the information she requested and only asked for the same street address. Four more companies popped up on the screen. And with those companies, the rest of the deposits to Ollie's account were matched.

"I'll bet," Zach said, "that Stephanie Norman handled all those bills."

Martin nodded. "I think that I'll go talk to the lady in question."

"She was nervous this afternoon, Martin, when I talked with her," Zach offered.

"I'll bet. If you'll print off copies for me, Toni, I'd like to confront Ms. Norman with this evidence."

Quickly, Toni produced the pages and Martin left.

When Zach returned to the study, he smiled at her. "You were a big help, Toni. Your knowledge made the difference."

She smiled. "It wasn't hard. I just knew how that system operated, and you didn't."

Zach grinned. "A smart man always knows when he's reached the limit of his knowledge and asks for help."

"And I believe you're a smart man."

Another chunk of the armor that shielded Zach's heart fell away. He didn't know what to do with himself. He felt as if he were standing naked before Toni and with a single thrust, she could wound him. He didn't like the feeling one bit, nor was he sure he could walk this road. "That remains to be seen." His voice sounded hard to his own ears. He noted that the animation on Toni's face faded. He felt like a monster for hurting her in that way.

She straightened her shoulders and met his gaze. "I need to go out to the aviary before we go to the party and check on the bird the girls and I treated the other day. I think Lori will want to go out with me."

As he watched Toni and Lori walk away, he felt two

inches tall. He glanced down to where Lisa rested her head on his leg. Her mouth twisted into a pout. "Those birds are okay, but I'd rather play with Sam." She looked up. "You don't have to be careful with him." She scampered to the dog. "C'mon, Sam, let's go play house."

Zach shook his head. He sat at the table and opened the newspaper. After a while, the phone rang and Zach picked it up.

"Zach, this is Martin. We're at Stephanie Norman's house. The lady has skipped town."

Zach mouthed a cursed. "So, we're still one step behind."

"It appears so."

Suddenly the scene with Carl Ormand talking to a blond woman in the parking lot of Anderson Oil the other day came to mind. Zach related the incident to the detective. "When I was talking to Stephanie today, I had the feeling that I'd met her before, yet I knew I hadn't. That accounts for the feeling. You might want to talk to Carl."

"You want to accompany me?" Martin asked.

"I'd like nothing better. Let me access the company's files and get the address." It only took a few minutes to get the information. "I'll meet you there in ten minutes."

Zach turned to race down to the aviary, when he saw Toni and Lori walking toward him. He quickly related what had happened to Toni.

"Martin and I are going to talk to Carl."

Toni studied him. "I doubt you'll get anything out of the man."

Zach's smile was wolfish. "I'd like to try."

"You'll be home in time for the party, won't you?"

"Yes." Zach knew there'd be hell to pay if he missed the reception.

As he drove to Carl's apartment, his words rang through his head. Maybe Toni did know him too well.

Martin stood beside his car, waiting for Zach. He parked behind the detective.

"Is Carl there?" Zach asked.

"His car is parked in the garage. If we're in luck, maybe we'll discover Stephanie in his house."

Zach shook his head. "I don't believe in fairy tales."

"I don't, either, but a little luck about now would be appreciated."

Martin knocked and the door quickly opened. Carl's expression was not welcoming. "Yes?"

"I'm Detective Martin Phelps of the Midland Police Department. I have some questions I'd like to ask you about the death of Ollie Townshed."

Carl glared at Zach. "What's he doing here?"

"Mr. Knight has been helpful in gathering information relating to this case. He's here at my request."

Carl stepped back and motioned the two men inside. Once settled in the living room, Martin asked, "Do you know Stephanie Norman?"

"I believe she works at Anderson." He tried to appear at ease, but the tightness in his jaw belied his act.

"Do you know her?" Martin pressed.

"No more than any other employee," Carl replied.

"Is that why you were having a heart-to-heart discussion with her in the parking lot several days ago?" Zach asked.

Carl nailed Zach with a glare. "The woman asked me for advice."

"And are you in the habit of advising all the personnel at the company?" Martin asked.

"No. But the woman had a problem and asked if I could help. It would've been rude to ignore her."

"What did she ask you about, Carl?" Zach pressed.

"I don't have to answer you," Carl snapped.

Zach's eyes narrowed and a muscle in his jaw flexed.

"That's true," Martin interjected. "But you do have to answer me. And I'd like to hear the answer to the question. What did Stephanie ask you about?"

"She asked about a noise she had in her engine. I told her to take it in and have a mechanic look it over."

Martin looked at Zach.

"So, what you're telling me is that you and Stephanie are casual acquaintances?"

"That's right."

Martin stood. "All right, Mr. Ormand. If I have any further questions, I'll contact you."

When they walked to their cars, Zach shook his head.

"The man is lying through his teeth."

"He sure is," Martin replied.

"So, what are we going to do?" Zach asked.

"We're going to try to locate Stephanie. She might be our key."

"Yeah, and I know where the locked door is," Zach answered, throwing a hard stare at Carl's house.

"Well, is Carl still alive and well?" Toni asked Zach and Martin as they walked into the house.

Martin smiled. "There was a moment there that I thought Zach was going to flatten the man."

"Too bad I didn't. We would've gotten more information out of him if I had."

"Zach, that kind of evidence would be thrown out

of court. If Carl is connected with the murder of Ollie Townshed and the gauger, then I want to do things by the book so we can lock him up.''

''Wait a minute. You think Carl murdered Ollie? And the gauger, too?'' Toni's gaze clashed with Zach's. He'd withheld important information from her. The knowledge knifed through her heart. Why hadn't Zach told her? She was his wife and intimately involved with Anderson.

''Let's go into the study,'' Martin said, ''and I'll tell you what we suspect has happened.''

Once they were seated, Martin began. ''You know that Ollie was swindling money from Anderson. We found evidence—company stationery, invoices, in his apartment—that suggested Ollie was Caprock. In his residence we also found the logbooks from the field where the gauger was killed. We think Ollie was somehow involved with that man's murder or knew who murdered him. But since Ollie is dead, we're going to have to piece together this connection without his help.''

Toni glanced at Zach. He hadn't told her the full story.

''So, to carry on this scam, there has to be someone in accounting letting his phony charges go through. We think that person was Stephanie Norman, who is now missing.''

''And what you're telling me is Stephanie might have knowledge of these two murders?'' Toni asked.

''She might,'' Zach answered. ''Or she might just be a minor peg in a bigger conspiracy. We need to find and question her.''

''Are you sure she's skipped town?'' Toni asked.

''No,'' Martin answered. ''But one of the neighbors

saw the lady go out to her car with a suitcase. I think it's likely that she won't show up at work tomorrow."

"I think I'll go back tomorrow and question the neighbors about Stephanie. Maybe they can identify a boyfriend and we can nail Carl that way." Martin glanced at his watch. "I'm sorry I stayed so late. I know y'all have a party to go to."

Zach walked Martin to his car.

Martin shook his head. "If I don't miss my guess, Toni was surprised by some of the information I told her."

A sigh escaped Zach. "Yeah, I guess she was."

"You didn't tell her everything that was going on? Even when she was the one who helped us discover that the Caprock billing statements matched Ollie's checkbook?"

It made him stop and think when Martin put it in those terms, but there had been valid reasons not to tell her. "I'm not used to working with anyone, Martin."

"You've shared with me," he stated.

Yeah, and he wasn't emotionally involved with Martin, either. "That's your job. And my job, to discover who was stealing from the company."

"But she's your wife and the daughter of the company president."

Those were two fine points that Zach couldn't discount. So, why hadn't he trusted her? "Let's just say that I've been married before and have become wary of trusting women."

Martin pinned him with a stare. "I think that your wife isn't going to buy that excuse." He shrugged. "But I wish you luck."

Zach watched as Martin pulled away. He rubbed his neck. He had to agree with Martin; he was in trouble with Toni. It had been plain in her eyes when her gaze rested on him. She felt she'd been the one wronged, when nothing he did had been out of order.

While Zach was gone, Toni made sure the girls were dressed in their best clothes for the reception tonight. When Zach walked back into the house, they were ready to leave.

"I'll put on a tie and be with you in a moment."

"We'll wait in the car for you, Zach," Toni told him. As they walked to the car, Zach realized how he had screwed up in the situation. If he didn't miss his guess, Toni wasn't going to forgive him any time soon.

Zach smiled as Toni chatted with an old friend, Fred Green. Fred was grinning from ear to ear.

"Your daddy was proud as punch when he told me about you marrying this fine young man. And those little girls are cute as newborn heifers. You must be proud of them, Zach."

He slipped his arm around Toni's waist and pulled her close. They wanted all of Midland to believe they married because of love. In spite of that, he felt Toni stiffen. Their earlier confrontation came to mind. "I am, indeed."

"So, Toni, is this going to keep you out of the fields this spring?" Fred asked.

"Nope, Fred. I'll still be out checking on the screens for the sludge tanks so the migrating birds don't land in them."

Fred scowled. "Now, Toni, you need to pay attention to your new family and not butt into everyone else's business."

"And you, Fred, need to make sure your screens are in place," she retorted.

"I bet you don't talk to your daddy that way!" Fred protested.

Toni laughed. "That's where you're wrong, Fred. Ask him. He claims I'm a pain. But he does see about the screens."

Zach watched in amazement as Toni faced down the oilman. The topic of screens on the sludge tanks had come up often tonight, and Toni hadn't backed down a single time. Oddly enough, the oilmen took her warning to heart. Her campaign had never been a popular one, even with her father. He also felt proud of how Toni stood up to the man.

"Everyone, let me have your attention," George yelled over the buzz of the room. When quiet reigned, he continued. "I want you to raise your champagne glasses in a toast to Toni and her husband, Zachary Knight. May their marriage be long and fruitful."

"Here, here," the response came.

"And I hope each of you will come by and greet my newest granddaughters," George continued, "Lisa and Lori." George pointed at each girl.

Zach was surprised and pleased by George's acknowledgement of the girls. Lisa beamed as she sipped her soft drink. Lori smiled shyly.

Watching George over the past few days with the girls gave Zach a totally different perspective on the gruff man. George assumed the role of adoring grandfather, which his girls ate up. It was a bonus Zach hadn't even thought about.

Fred's wife joined the group.

"Toni," Claudia said, "I was so shocked to hear on the news tonight about Ollie Townshed being found dead in the trunk of his car. You must be shocked."

Toni's eyes met Zach's. So, the death had made the

news. They'd been so busy checking on the fraud at the company that they had ignored the local news. But maybe Stephanie Norman had heard the news and that was the reason she skipped town.

Toni shook her head. ''It's a shock to us all, Claudia.''

''Well, my dear, I hope the police can solve that murder and quickly.''

''We all do.''

''It was so nice to meet your new husband. Congratulations.'' The tone in which Claudia said it made it sound as if no one expected Toni to ever marry and that they were surprised that she had. Zach resented the woman's attitude and frowned. Claudia pulled Fred away to meet the girls.

''The old bat,'' Zach grumbled under his breath.

Surprise colored Toni's eyes. When she met his gaze, Zach gave her an unrepentant look. The corner of her mouth twitched.

Zach was aware that there was still a gulf between them, the one he'd put there, and one he didn't doubt that he'd hear about once they were alone. They shared the moment, but it quickly disappeared.

The rest of the evening passed in much the same manner, many of the individuals expressing surprise, subtly and not so subtly, at Toni's sudden marriage. Zach knew that because Lisa and Lori's future depended on his performance, he smiled and kept his arm around Toni's waist. But she never relaxed against him as she had this afternoon.

Finally, after ninety minutes of torture, Toni made the excuse that the girls were tired and needed to go home. The drive back there was made in silence. With each mile, Zach noted that Toni became more anxious.

Once at the house, they carried the girls to their bedroom. As Zach helped Lori into her nightgown, Toni paused. "I can do this." He knew that she wanted to be rid of him. Perversely, he smiled.

"It will be quicker if I help."

Never had an offer of help been greeted with such aversion.

Without talking to him, Toni finished getting Lisa ready for bed. After she kissed both girls, Toni walked out of the room. Zach let her go.

Once in their room, Toni shed her clothes and hopped into the shower. She hoped a hot shower would relieve some of the tension in her muscles.

He hadn't trusted her. The refrain rang over and over in her mind all night long. Each time she'd said it to herself this evening, the hurt and anger increased. What made the situation even worse was having to stand by Zach all night, feel his hand on her waist, and play the loving couple. She'd felt like a fraud. And then on the ride home, Zach had acted as if nothing had happened.

After she stepped out of the shower, dried herself off and slipped into her robe, she looked at herself in the mirror.

Her eyes were dark with hurt. His lack of confidence in her was like a knife in her heart.

Her heart broke, along with the dreams she'd been spinning.

After he checked the doors and windows, Zach stopped by the girls' door. They were asleep. Sam was between the girls and Lisa had her leg thrown over Sam's back. Two months ago he couldn't have imagined this scenario in his wildest dream. His life had changed so dramatically, he was still groping to find his way.

But Toni had helped.

So, had he blown it by not trusting her? That was the question he had wrestled with all night at the reception. The guilt and confusion.

No, dammit, he hadn't been wrong in his actions, he finally convinced himself, staring at the girls. He'd been only going on what he knew and experienced.

When he stepped into their bedroom, Toni came out of the bathroom. Her wet hair left wet spots on her robe. She didn't look at him, but went to the dresser and pulled out a nightgown. As she turned to go back into the bathroom, Zach caught her arm.

"Toni, we need to talk," he began lamely.

Her gaze went to his hand on her arm. He released her and stepped back.

"Why, Zach?" Hurt darkened her eyes.

He didn't answer.

"Tonight, it became perfectly clear that you don't trust me and only gave me enough information so I could solve your problems. Am I wrong, Zach, in my assessment of the situation?" Her gaze bore into his.

He couldn't lie to her. "No."

"I thought not, so what have I missed?"

"I wanted to explain to you why I kept some details from you."

She crossed her arms under her breasts and waited for him to explain.

"Toni, you know that there's been no one outside my unit in the military who I've trusted. The women in my life didn't inspire those feelings in me. My mother— Well it's best if I don't say anything there.

My ex-wife, she enjoyed sharing with her lover what I had told her during and after our lovemaking. It was hard to hear my words out of the mouth of another man who'd slept with my wife. She, most of all, shattered what little illusions I had about women.''

He rubbed his neck. ''And I'll admit I wasn't a monk after my divorce, but there's been no one I felt I could trust.''

Toni's expression softened. ''I understand that, Zach, but I'm not your mother nor your first wife nor a casual woman in your life. You'll have to judge me on myself, not on the sins of another.''

Her words hit him hard, angering him. ''Are you telling me that you don't judge me against that SOB to whom you were engaged?''

''Touché, Zach.'' She took a deep steadying breath. ''I started by comparing you with him. But somewhere along the way, what he did faded away, and I only saw you. Can you say the same?''

Her last remark hit him dead center, making him flinch inside. ''I'll sleep in the spare bedroom, tonight.''

''That would probably be a good idea.''

As he walked from the room, Toni's stricken expression haunted him throughout the night.

Chapter 13

Toni glanced in the bathroom mirror and touched up her makeup. The dark circles under her eyes were a mute witness to the sleepless night she'd spent. She'd reached out several times in those hours to find Zach's warmth and his reassuring strength but only found emptiness. Odd, how quickly she'd become accustomed to having him sleep beside her.

But each time she'd felt the urge to go to him, she remembered how he hadn't trusted her. Apparently, she'd been good enough to care for his children, good enough to sleep with, but not good enough to entrust with all the information about the thefts at *her* dad's company. What she wanted from Zach was a partnership, a giving and taking. Trust. Not just good sex. Although—

When she walked out of the bathroom, Lisa was sitting on the bed, her nightgown bunched around her knees, her legs swinging off the mattress.

"Why's Daddy sleeping in the other room?" Her earnest expression touched Toni's heart.

Toni sat beside her. "Why do you ask?"

"'Cause I saw him walking out of that bedroom—" she pointed to the room across the hall "—with a bad frown on his face. I didn't want to ask him when he had that mad look."

Toni pulled Lisa close. "Do you and Lori fight?" Toni questioned.

"Yeah, but we always make up. Sometimes, Lori acts really icky and makes me mad. Then we fight." Lisa leaned back. "Did that happen to you and Daddy?"

The innocence of childhood, what a blessing. "That's what happened, Lisa. Your daddy and I got cross with each other."

"But you're going to make up, aren't you?"

Toni heard the note of fear in Lisa's voice.

"I think so."

"Is that a yes or no?"

The child wanted assurances, ones she didn't have the right to make, but would. "Yes."

"Good. I'm hungry. Can we eat now?"

"Why don't you and your sister get dressed, then we'll eat."

Toni watched Lisa walk away and decided that she would try her best to make the promise to Lisa come true.

As Toni helped the girls to dress, she was able to look at the situation between her and Zach without the pain of betrayal clouding the view. Perhaps she had expected too much of him. She'd wanted perfection. What he'd given her was a beginning. He'd trusted her with a good deal of the information they'd uncovered.

He'd tried.

That thought made her pause. He'd tried. And hadn't he changed from that reserved, self-contained man that she originally knew to a man who was affectionate with his children? And her?

Maybe things weren't so black as they had appeared last night.

A ray of hope sprang to life in her heart.

When she and the girls entered the kitchen after they were dressed, Zach stood by the coffeemaker, a cup in his hand. He'd cut grapefruit for everyone.

From the haggard look of his face, Zach hadn't spent any more restful a night than she had. Perhaps he'd been plagued with doubts and remorse as she had been.

"I would've done the scrambled eggs, but—" He shrugged.

"Ick, Daddy," Lisa commented. "Don't do that. Let Mommy. She does it better."

He didn't smile, but a warmth crept into his eyes. "You're right, Lisa. She does it better."

It was a compliment, and Toni didn't think Zach was talking about eggs.

"He's dead, Carl." Stephanie's fear-filled eyes met Carl's.

He wanted to shout at her for running like she had. He was lucky he remembered about the farmhouse. He wouldn't do anything to spook her now. Traveling with her would make him less conspicuous. Everyone would think they were vacationing.

"He was going to ruin it for us, Stephanie. He'd gotten squeamish." Carl ran his hands through his hair. Everyone was turning chicken on him. He couldn't count on a single one. No one knew why he wanted to bleed that stupid company dry. He was meant to be the next successor as president of Anderson Oil. Except that the stupid broad dropped him after the incident at the Christmas party.

Oh, maybe, he shouldn't have come on the way he had, but the dumb woman didn't cooperate. Maybe it was better this way. He got a thrill each time he had Stephanie submit a false billing. It was better than sex. It certainly was better than sex with Stephanie.

"What are we going to do?" she asked, her eyes filled with worry.

"Leave."

"What?" Stephanie looked like a landed trout, eyes glassy and mouth open.

"We'll leave today, after I go back and get the money and the numbers of the accounts."

"I don't want to leave," Stephanie protested.

Carl's hand lashed out and he struck her across the cheek. "There's no choice."

Fear entered her eyes.

"Is there?" he asked.

"No," she whispered.

He smiled and lightly kissed her bruised cheek. "I'll be back in a couple of hours. Be ready to go."

As Carl drove back to Midland, he began to whistle and tried to come up with ways he could kill Stephanie once they were in Mexico.

Zach glared at June Davis. He knew he was in his intimidating-soldier mode, but he couldn't put a lid on it. "Do you know where Stephanie could be?"

The woman bristled and drew herself up to her five-foot-two-inch height. "Ms. Norman didn't call this morning, notifying us of her absence. Since I am not her mother, I didn't call or go to her house. Mothering is not in my job description.'' The look in her eyes would've done his old drill sergeant proud.

A sigh escaped his throat. ''Do you have any idea where she might be?''

''I don't make it a habit to know my employees' lives.'' The woman's attitude rang with hostility. ''Now, if you'll excuse me, I have work to do,'' she snapped and marched off.

Zach looked around the room to where the other accounting employees sat. From their closed looks, he knew he wouldn't get any information there.

As he walked back to his office, he cursed himself for having the tactical approach of a bull elephant on the scent of a female. If he'd thought for a moment, before going in there with guns blazing, he might have gotten June to cooperate. His only excuse was his mind had been preoccupied. And what had his mind been consumed with?

Toni.

He had tried all through the night to come to grips with what had happened yesterday. Although he'd thought Toni didn't have any right to be angry with him about withholding information, he had to look at the situation honestly. Finally, in the early hours of the morning, he decided she might have a point.

So, where did that leave him? He hadn't ever had a reason to trust—until now. But could he rely on the new feelings that Toni stirred in his heart, or would it end in disaster again?

He'd done what he thought was right and kept this case close to his vest. His head and heart were sending him conflicting messages and, as of yet, he hadn't resolved the discrepancy.

As he walked down the hall, he noticed that Carl's door was closed. He turned the handle and discovered the door locked.

"He hasn't come in yet, Mr. Knight," the woman from the neighboring office informed Zach as she walked out into the hall.

"How do you know?" he asked.

"Because there have been several people who needed to speak to Mr. Ormand this morning. They usually end up in my office, asking about him."

"Thanks."

So, now he had both Carl and Stephanie missing. He was ready to put his fist through a wall when he walked into his office and found Toni.

"Did you forget our appointment with the social worker at ten this morning?" Toni asked.

His eyes widened, then he mouthed a word not fit for proper company. Glancing at his watch, he saw they had fifteen minutes to get to the social worker's office.

"I'm ready to go."

As they walked to his car, Toni reminded him, "Don't growl at the woman. It won't help your chances if you do."

At this point, he wouldn't bet a nickel on his chances.

Amazingly enough, Zach attempted to answer Francis Getty's question.

"No, it wasn't an amiable divorce. Once Sylvia left me, I never saw her again. I got the divorce papers in the mail. I was on a mission when the court hearing was held. I didn't object to anything she claimed. She didn't ask for support. She just wanted out."

"Why didn't you object?"

"I wasn't a good husband. When the initial attraction wore off, Sylvia and I didn't have anything in common. I focused on my job in Special Forces, while Sylvia went looking for other men. She needed attention. Constant attention."

Francis eyed him. "She was unfaithful to you?"

"She was."

"And you're sure that the girls are your biological children?"

"When the social worker in Phoenix called me, I was shocked and sure I wasn't the father—that it was a bad joke. I submitted to a paternity test in Phoenix and it came back, confirming me as the father. And then when I laid eyes on the girls, I knew they were mine."

"What makes you think you can raise these children?" Francis pressed.

"Because, Ms. Getty, I'm committed to them. No matter what else happens, I'm the girls' father."

When he added the information about his own childhood, how he'd been abandoned, Toni thought she saw a softening of the woman's attitude.

"All right," Francis said, "since the girls have been with you awhile, tell me what the girls like to eat."

He was honest. "Nothing that I've cooked, but they love my wife's cooking."

Toni seconded Zach's observation. "That's the truth. The girls beg Zach not to try to cook."

Francis smothered a smile.

"Lisa is the talkative one. Lori is quieter." He explained about their love of Sam and burying the fish in the flower garden.

At the end of the interview, Francis told them she'd

write a report and submit it to the court. They'd get a copy.

"I think you impressed Francis with your answers," Toni said as they drove back to Anderson.

"I tried to be honest."

"I know you did, Zach."

He glanced at her. Their argument from last night rang through his head, and he wanted to reexplain to Toni why he'd done what he had. He wasn't successful the first time he'd tried, and he doubted he'd be any more successful a second time. So, where did that leave him?

"Carl isn't at work today," he said instead. The words popped out of his mouth before he could think.

"Do you think he's with Stephanie?" Toni asked.

"It sure looks like it. I just wish I knew where to look for those two."

"Why don't you stop by Carl's house before we go back? That way we can see why he's not at work."

"That's an excellent idea." He detoured to Carl's house. There was no one home, and Carl's car wasn't in the garage. When Zach got back into the car, he said, "He's not there, and I'll bet if we locate Stephanie, we'll find Carl."

Zach's words stayed in Toni's mind the rest of the way back to Anderson. When they got there, Zach went back to his office. Instead of going to her car, Toni walked to the lunchroom. Several of the ladies from accounting, with whom she'd spent a lot of time, were sitting together, chatting over their lunch.

Toni strolled up to the group. "Hello," she called out the greeting. "Mind if I join you?"

Sarah Early waved Toni to a seat next to her. "Come sit here, and we can talk about your new husband."

For the next ten minutes, the women caught up on old information. Children and grandchildren. Zach.

"You could've knocked me over with a feather when I heard about that," Sharon Williams said. "I never would've thought that that stone-faced man would have children and get married." She glanced at Toni. "I'm sorry," she murmured, her face turning a blotchy red. "I mean—"

"That's okay, Sharon," Toni interrupted. "I understand that Zach is a bit reserved and at other times he's very intimidating."

"Of course, you should've seen him this morning with June." Sharon shook her hand. "Whoa, not only can our supervisor take it, that woman sure can dish it out. I thought Zach was going to blow a gasket."

"What were they arguing about?" Toni asked.

Delores Taylor smiled, then leaned closer. "Your husband wanted to know about Stephanie. June said she wasn't her mother."

Toni's eyes widened, then laughter erupted from her mouth. The women returned her humor with smiles and chuckles.

"I suspect Zach will walk softly around June from now on, just like my dad does." She glanced around the table. "Ladies, I do need your help. We think Stephanie might be the key to some of the swindling that's been going on in the company."

The women exchanged glances.

"I thought something was up yesterday when June got hot under the collar about some billing," Delores added, fiddling with her salad.

"It appears that Stephanie has skipped town. Zach and the police want to try to find her to question her.

Do any of you have any idea where she might have gone?''

"She was an only child," Delores offered. "Her mom passed away a couple of months ago."

"Do you know where her mother lived?" Toni asked.

Sharon, Delores and Sarah looked at each other.

"It was somewhere close. A little town…" Delores said.

Sarah frowned. "Some place like Nowhere, or No-place or—"

"Notrees," Sharon offered.

"Yes, that's it," Sarah added.

"Where's that?" Toni asked.

"It's northwest of here on a state highway—I don't remember exactly where, but it's within fifty miles." Sharon shrugged. "It should be easy to find on a map."

"Was she dating anyone in particular? I mean, did she talk about her boyfriend? Or her dates?"

Delores smiled. "Stephanie was very closemouthed about her love life, and we all doubted that she had one. Then about a year ago Christmas, Stephanie comes in, with this cat-ate-the-canary smile and announces she has a boyfriend. When we asked about the man, Stephanie wouldn't talk about him. All we knew was that he was very important and depended on her."

"She acted like she was superior to the rest of us in the department," Sharon added. "Finally, we all stopped asking about her mystery man. I think Stephanie was disappointed we didn't make a bigger stink about it."

"Any man you can't or don't introduce to friends and co-workers," Delores added, "isn't worth spit. It's my guess he was married."

"Or doing something illegal," Sharon added.

The information fit in with what Zach and she already knew. "Thanks, ladies," Toni said, smiling at each woman. "I'll be sure to let you know what happened."

"Toni," Delores added, "we all want to congratulate you."

Toni smiled and nodded. Too bad her heart was so heavy.

Zach looked up when Toni entered his office. He was surprised that she was still here at Anderson.

"I've got a lead on Stephanie Norman."

Resting his elbows on the desk, he leaned forward. "What is it, and where did you discover it?"

"Are you going to cop an attitude with me, Zach? I could give this information to Detective Phelps." She started to turn around.

"Sorry." He ran his fingers through his hair. "What did you find out?"

"I decided to talk to some of my old friends in accounting. They were very helpful with information about Stephanie."

"Oh." The look of doubt on Zach's face provoked her.

"Yes, it appears that Stephanie acquired a new high-powered boyfriend around Christmas last year."

His eyes narrowed. "Just about the time I punched out Carl?"

"That's right. She kept the name of this man a secret but bragged about what a find he was. After a while, when Stephanie didn't reveal his name, the ladies quit asking about him. But apparently, Stephanie continued to see the man."

Rubbing his chin, Zach asked, "Did they give you any idea where she might be?"

"Her mother—who recently passed away—lived in Notrees."

A frown wrinkled his brow. "Where's that?"

"We need to pull out a map. It's somewhere northwest of here."

It only took a few seconds for Zach to locate a map. The town was in the next county, northwest of Odessa.

"I think it's worth a try to see if she's there," Zach said, folding up the map.

"Do you want to go now?" Toni asked.

Zach's gaze narrowed. "I hadn't planned to take anyone with me."

From his reaction, Toni knew Zach wasn't used to being questioned or allowing others to do his job. But that didn't change a thing. He was going to need her help.

"Well, maybe you should rethink your strategy. From the reaction you had with June this morning and Stephanie yesterday, you should probably have someone with you who isn't so intimidating. I think Stephanie would be more willing to talk to me instead of you."

A frown creased his mouth.

"Zach, we both want to discover what's going on. And I think I'm going to be the best bet to talk to Stephanie, if we find her."

It was obvious that he didn't like the idea of taking her with him, but he continued to study her. After several long moments, he nodded.

"You've got a point." He sighed. "All right, let's go to Notrees." He stood. "Do you have any appointments or classes this afternoon?"

"Nope, my schedule is clear."

"What about the girls?"

Toni glanced down at her watch. It was close to one. The girls had to be picked up by three. "Let's stop by my dad's office. He can get the girls. I think Dad and Lisa and Lori will enjoy the experience. Isn't it a good thing that I put Dad on the permission form for the preschool?"

Zach didn't look convinced, but he didn't say anything.

When they entered George's office, he was talking on the phone. He motioned them inside. When he finished the call, he turned to Toni.

"What are you doing here?" George asked.

"Dad, Zach and I are going on an errand. We might not be back in time to get the girls. Will you do that?"

George nailed Zach with a look. "Where are you going? Does this trip have anything to do with the missing woman in accounting?"

Toni turned to Zach. "How does he know about Stephanie?"

"He told me," George answered.

A sadness swept over Toni. Obviously Zach had informed her dad of everything that had happened. He'd trusted George enough with the information, but not her. And although reason told her Zach hadn't been obligated to inform her, she wanted that trust.

But that's his job, reason answered.

"You found her?" George look at Zach.

"Not yet." Zach looked at Toni. "Toni talked to some of the ladies in accounting, and they told her where we might find Stephanie."

"Where is she?" George asked.

"They told Toni about a place her mother had in

Notrees. We're going to try it. Also, she discovered that Stephanie had an important boyfriend, whom she acquired last Christmas, right around the time the false billings started.''

"We think that man was Carl," Toni added.

George looked at his daughter, then Zach. "Why was Toni the one who uncovered this information, Zach, instead of you?"

"I tried talking to June in accounting this morning. She wasn't helpful." Frustration laced Zach's voice.

"She took a chunk out of you, did she, boy?" George's eyebrow shot up.

Zach shook his head. "It was stupid of me to challenge her like I did. I won't do it again."

"Well, don't feel bad. June cut me off at the knees several years ago when I questioned why she hadn't paid a particular supplier. The problem was, I didn't submit the bill my friend gave me." He shrugged. "It happens to the best of us. But I'll tell you, I walk carefully around that woman."

Zach stared at George. "Why do you keep her?"

"Because she's the best damn manager I have. She's saved my bacon on more than one occasion. I'm lucky she hasn't left for greener pastures." He looked at Toni. "I'll get the girls. And maybe I'll take the girls to see their new aunt in Saddle. I think your sister Alex might like to see Lisa and Lori again."

Toni leaned down and kissed her dad. "Thanks."

As they were leaving the office, George called out, "Cheer up, Zach. Better men than you have been taken down by June."

As they drove to Notrees, Zach frowned at the road. He wanted to explain to Toni why he'd kept her father updated. It was his job, and if she didn't understand that, then maybe anything he would try to do for Toni would fall short.

"Zach, I realize that it was your job to keep my dad informed. I also know if you hadn't, he would've chewed you up and spit you out. I know that in my head. It's my heart that's putting up the fuss." She glanced at him. "Only my feelings aren't obeying my mind. But I'm going to ignore the feelings and go with what my brain is saying."

He wanted to shake his head to make sure he'd heard right. "Are you telling me you understand?" Disbelief rang in his voice. Never had he had a reaction like that before from a woman.

"I'm telling you that I'm trying." She shrugged. "I guess I need time."

Her words floored him. He was tempted to pull over to the side of the road, stop the car and have her say it again just to make sure. Whatever he'd been expecting from Toni, her reasonable response wasn't it. His first wife would've been screaming her head off, accusing him of all sorts of evil things. He knew how to deal with that drill. He didn't have the foggiest notion of what to do now or how to respond.

A chuckle escaped her lips.

Again her reaction blindsided him. "What's so funny?" he asked, his curiosity prodding him.

"I was just imagining you and June squaring off, toe-to-toe. It must've been an awesome sight."

His mouth curved into a self-deprecating smile as he remembered the encounter. "Well, she certainly surprised me. I didn't know she was that—"

"Tough?" Toni suggested.

That was a nice way to put it. "Yeah. Does she have

a nickname, such as the Terminator or Maneater? Or maybe she's related to General Patton.''

"Not that I know of, but when I worked for Dad, I wasn't privy to the juiciest gossip. That could've had something to do with who my dad was.''

He didn't doubt that. He hadn't considered what her life had been growing up. She was the youngest child of a very wealthy man who apparently had caused a big scandal in Midland. "What was it like growing up with George as your father?''

"That's kind of hard to explain.'' She glanced out over the flat landscape. "I never wanted for anything. And I never doubted for a minute my folks loved me. But...I always wondered why people whispered when my dad was around. Apparently, everyone remembered the scandal. But no one ever said anything to my dad's or mom's face. I was told by a playmate what my dad had done. When I asked him about it, Dad looked me straight in the eye and said it was true. He owned up to the fact he'd been wrong. But, he told me he'd gotten two wonderful daughters.''

She shook her head. "Things changed when J.D.'s mother died and J.D. came to live with us. Amazingly, J.D. didn't hate my mom, Alex or me. I think she was mad at Dad, but she decided that she was going to be so good in school, Dad would be proud of her.''

"And was he proud of her?'' Zach asked.

"Do you need to ask?''

From the pictures of his children and grandchildren in his office, Zach knew the answer. "I think he was.''

"And in spite of his faults, Dad was there for me when I was in the accident. He's the reason I made it through.'' Her eyes grew moist. "It's said that love covers a multitude of sins. It's true, Zach. Love can make the difference in a situation, if you survive or don't.''

He didn't know if he believed her. There certainly hadn't been an excess of love in his life.

And maybe that was the problem.

She shook her head. "J.D. had the same problem as the rest of us. There was no man good enough for us. Oh, he did want us to get married, but when push came to shove, I think Dad got cold feet.

"And when Rafe showed up, I thought my dad would explode from the delight and pride. Rafe was ready to hate Dad, but seeing Dad's reaction, him beaming and introducing Rafe to everyone we knew, Rafe didn't stand a chance. Dad overwhelmed him, like he does everyone else.''

Zach was still blown away by George's reaction. Neither of his parents cared a whit about him. He could've drowned before their eyes, and neither one would've lifted a finger to help him. It was a bitterness that had driven him long and hard.

Suddenly, watching Lisa and Lori, seeing them blossom before his eyes, the edge of that ugliness was blunted.

Maybe the woman beside him had something to do with that. And he wanted to reach out and claim what he'd found. Would it last? Could he trust it?

The thought made him edgy.

Chapter 14

Notrees consisted of a gas station, a feed store and a post office. Zach stopped for gas. When he went inside to pay for his purchase, he asked, "I'm looking for the Norman house. Where would I find it?"

The old man behind the counter studied Zach. "Mrs. Norman died a couple of months ago."

"I'm looking for her daughter. I thought she might be at the residence."

"Can't say if Stephanie's there, but their place is two miles west on sixty-nine. You know, you're the second stranger today who has asked about the Norman place."

"Tell me, was the other stranger a man about six foot, blond hair and a scar on his chin?" Zach asked.

"Yeah, that's him." The old man snorted. "In a mighty big hurry, too. Bad manners. Didn't even say thanks."

"When did this man ask about the Norman ranch?"

"Early this morning."

"Thanks for the information." Zach hurried back to his car.

"Did you discover where the house is?" Toni asked.

"I did. And I also discovered that Carl's ahead of us."

"How?"

"The gentleman in the gas station told me I was the second person to ask after the Norman place. The other man was Carl."

Zach zipped out of town and raced to the turnoff to the Norman ranch. The gravel road bounced the car as he sped toward the ranch house. He parked behind an older sedan and reached over to pull out the gun in the glove compartment. He quickly checked it, making sure it was loaded.

"What are you doing?" Toni asked.

"I'm taking precautions. I don't know what Carl's up to, or even if he's here, but I'm not going anywhere without this." He didn't put the weapon down, but kept it in his hand.

As they walked to the front door, Zach glanced around the yard and beyond. He didn't see any other cars and wondered if Carl was still here. For a split second, he feared they were going to find another dead body. He'd bet money that Carl had killed the gauger and Ollie.

Zach knocked on the door. The drapes covering the front window rippled, then the door opened a crack.

"What do you want?" Fear and hostility laced Stephanie's voice.

Toni stepped to where the woman could see her. "Why don't you let Zach and me come inside, Stephanie, and we can talk?"

The woman inside looked around the area.

"Stephanie, we know about the false billing you've done," Toni added. "I think it would be in your best interest to talk to us and help yourself."

The animosity in her eyes died, to be replaced by dismay. She stepped back and opened the door.

"Are you alone?" Zach asked before they entered.

"Yes." She turned around and walked back into the living room.

Not trusting her, Zach cautiously entered the room. When he only saw Stephanie, he motioned for Toni to enter.

"Why don't you talk to her, while I check the rest of the house?" Zach whispered.

Toni nodded and sat next to Stephanie. It was then that Toni noticed the swelling on Stephanie's cheek.

"Did Carl hit you?" Toni quietly asked.

Stephanie's head came up and she stared at Toni.

"I know he's capable of the violence. He tried assaulting me, but my husband—" Toni nodded to where Zach disappeared "—stopped him."

Stephanie stared down at her hands. "He was so wonderful when we started dating. He brought me roses and perfume, and funny stuffed animals." She glanced up, her eyes beseeching Toni to understand. "I never had a boyfriend before."

Toni rested her hand on Stephanie's, giving a gentle squeeze. "When did Carl ask you to do the false billings?" Toni asked.

"It happened just after we made love the first time. I was a virgin, and I wanted to keep Carl." She shrugged. "The first time he asked, it was only for a few hundred dollars. I told myself it wouldn't matter to a company like Anderson."

Toni's heart went out to the young woman. Carl had cruelly used Stephanie and the reality of that truth must've hurt her. "But it didn't stop there, did it, Stephanie?"

"No. Carl and Ollie submitted a lot of false bills. They had me send all the payments to that mail center." Stephanie's eyes filled with tears. "I was caught as surely as Ollie, because I'd done the billings."

Zach heard the questions Toni asked. After satisfying himself that Carl wasn't hiding in a closet, he walked back to the living room.

"What made you run, Stephanie?" Zach asked.

Her frightened eyes shifted to him. "I heard about Ollie's murder on TV the day you came to the accounting department. I knew that Carl must've killed Ollie, so I left to come here. Carl followed me. When I asked him if he murdered Ollie, he said Ollie wanted out."

"Why did he hit you?" Toni asked.

"When he told me we were going to leave, I told him I didn't want to go. He slapped me, and I knew I had better agree with him. He went back for his passport and money."

"Was that this morning?" Zach asked.

Her eyes shifted nervously from Zach to her hands. "Yes. He'll probably be back soon."

Toni lightly touched Stephanie's hand. "Can you live with a man, Stephanie, wondering if he's going to kill you, then leave your body behind, like he did to Ollie?"

"And it's likely that Carl murdered Wayne Thompson, too. You'll just be another victim in a long line of people. It gets easier to kill each time," Zach told her.

"He wouldn't do that," Stephanie protested, but there was no sincerity in her voice.

Toni's eyes captured Stephanie's. "You don't believe that any more than I do. Maybe Ollie wanted out after the murder of Wayne, and Carl didn't like Ollie's cold feet."

"If I don't miss my guess, I think your Carl has already killed two people. Your odds aren't looking good, Stephanie, of living too long if you go with Carl."

Fear and desperation entered her eyes. "What do you want me to do?"

"Come with us to the Midland police and tell them what you know," Zach answered.

Her battle was clearly reflected in her eyes. Finally, she nodded her head.

Toni grasped her hand. "You're doing the right thing," she assured Stephanie.

"Why didn't he love me?" Stephanie asked, despair coloring her voice.

Toni couldn't ignore the young woman's pain. "It wasn't you, Stephanie. It was Carl. He's the type of man who's only interested in himself and what everyone can do for him."

"He didn't have kind words for you," Stephanie softly added.

Toni's eyebrow rose. "That I don't doubt."

Looking at Zach, Toni asked, "Do you want to call Martin and tell him we found Stephanie, and that she's willing to talk?"

"Yeah, I want to do that."

While Zach made the phone call, Stephanie retrieved her purse. As Toni waited, she paced the length of the living room. Her nerves were strung so tightly, that she thought she might snap. This seemed too easy. Finally, both Zach and Stephanie joined her.

"Martin is waiting for us. As soon as Stephanie gives her statement, they'll arrest Carl."

Zach opened the front door and glanced outside. Everything seemed quiet. He motioned Toni and Stephanie outside. As Stephanie passed in front of Zach, a shot rang out and Stephanie fell. Toni lunged forward as she screamed out Zach's name, then she felt the bullet rip into her side. She heard Zach bellow, then heard the shots he returned.

Within seconds, he knelt at her side. "Hold on, sweetheart. I'm going to call for help."

The burning in her side consumed her. It seemed like hours, but Zach returned and grasped her hand.

"Help's coming."

She looked up, and in his eyes, there was a tenderness Toni had longed to see. It was the last thing she remembered before blackness swallowed her.

The helicopter lifted off, carrying Toni and Stephanie to the hospital in Midland. The few minutes that it had taken for the helicopter to arrive at their location were the longest, most torturous of Zach's life. Countless times he replayed seeing Carl's gun appear over the far back fender of Zach's car, then Stephanie and Toni falling. As he reviewed it, it became obvious to Zach that Toni had lunged in front of him, taking the bullet surely meant for him.

A cold, reasoning anger washed over Zach, and he wished he could've put those slugs into Carl before he shot. Why hadn't he seen Carl hiding behind his car?

The county sheriff and Texas Rangers broke into his dark thoughts.

"We'll need to interview you about what happened here," the sheriff said.

"No problem. First, I'll need to call my wife's father and let him know what's happened."

"I can do that," one of the deputies volunteered.

Zach pinned the young man with a cold stare. "My wife's father is George Anderson."

The deputy's eyes widened and he looked at his superior in dismay.

"Why don't you let Mr. Knight call," the sheriff offered.

Zach nodded, walked inside, and made the call. After a few tries, Zach tracked George down in Saddle, where he'd taken the girls to visit his daughter. Amazingly enough, George took the news calmly, wanting the details of the incident.

"They're taking Toni to Midland Memorial. She should be there in minutes. Stephanie Norman is also on that chopper. Carl is dead. I was too late to stop him from shooting Toni."

"But you killed the SOB," George replied.

"I aimed for the heart."

"I wish you'd shot the bastard before he harmed my daughter."

"You're not the only one." It would be a regret he would always live with. "I have to finish talking to the sheriff and the Rangers, George. It might take me several hours here."

"We'll take the helicopter back and be expecting you."

When Zach hung up, he took a deep breath. He could only pray his session with the authorities was short. He needed to get to the hospital.

* * *

The drive from Notrees back to Midland was sheer hell. He went over every word that Toni had said on the way there in his head. She'd tried to understand why he hadn't trusted her enough with important information and had given him the benefit of the doubt. She had tried to understand why he acted as he had. That was a unique experience for him.

And what about how Toni had taken his children to heart? She loved the girls, done what she could for them. Lori had bloomed under Toni's tender care. Lisa was also thriving.

He, too, had felt the results of her love.

Looking at his own heart, Zach realized that he loved Toni. Odd, for a man who thought the notion of love was something teenage girls and songwriters said existed. Now, he knew that he'd been wrong. There was such a thing as love, because he felt it firsthand.

He prayed that he would have the chance to tell her.

When he walked into the operating waiting room, Lisa and Lori cried out his name and ran into his arms.

As he looked over the girls' heads, he saw George Anderson stand. Beside him sat his eldest daughter, J.D., and his son, Rafe.

"Oh, Daddy, is Momma goin' to be okay?" Lori asked, her face stained with tears.

Zach's gaze came back to his daughter. "I don't know, sweetheart." He stood and addressed George. "Have you heard anything?"

"No. Alex has gone to see about Toni." He looked at Zach. "Guess it's good to have a doctor in the family."

"Yeah…" Zach gave his daughters a hug.

"How did the interviews go with the police?" George asked.

"Fine. The Ranger took Carl's gun to see if it was the murder weapon in Ollie's murder. We think it was. It was the same caliber as the other murder weapon."

George nodded.

They sat for several more minutes before Alex and the surgeon walked in.

Zach shot to his feet. "How is she?"

The surgeon stepped forward. "Are you the husband?"

"I am."

"Your wife has lost a lot of blood, but we were able to repair the damage done by the bullet. We had to remove the spleen. She's critical at this point, but her prognosis is good. She's in recovery now. When we put her in intensive care, you can see her."

A weight was taken off Zach's shoulders.

"Is Momma goin' to be okay?" Lisa asked.

Zach looked down at his daughter. "We think so."

Lisa frowned. "Is that a yes?"

Alex scooped up Lisa and carried her into the hallway. He heard her murmur to the little girl. "Your momma was hurt by a bullet. We've fixed her up. Now all we can do is pray."

"Why did this happen?" Lisa cried.

Zach heard Alex comfort his daughter. Lori sat on George's lap, her head resting on his shoulder. Zach looked at each of these people and realized that he wasn't alone to face this tragedy. He had a family. The girls had a family, people to offer them comfort and support. It didn't all rest on his shoulders. It was an odd and unique experience for him. Family. He just hoped the most vital part of the family would make it.

* * *

When Zach walked into the intensive care unit, Toni was pale and hooked to several monitors. He walked to the head of the bed and lightly brushed his fingers across her cheek. Toni's eyes fluttered open.

"Hi," she murmured.

"Hi, yourself," Zach answered. "How do you feel?"

"Like I've been shot."

He smiled.

"How are the girls?" she asked.

"Worried about their new mother, just like their daddy is. Fight, Toni. We need you." His eyes held hers, and he tried to will her to get well.

"I will. I have too much to live for."

Zach sat holding Toni's hand. She'd made it out of intensive care to a private room. He was waiting for her to wake up.

Alex had recommended that Zach talk to Toni, telling her about the girls and anything he could think about.

"The girls are wanting to come and see you. The hospital won't let them up here, so your sisters are keeping them company. Alex took Lori to the doctor and she had her cast removed. She wanted to talk to you about it. She also wanted to know who was going to care for Bob, the Canada goose you have in the aviary."

"Call the department secretary. She has the name of a person to take care of the bird," Toni whispered.

Zach's eyes flew to Toni's face. Her eyes fluttered open and she tried to smile at him.

"It was a good story about Lori." Her voice was weak, but the sweetest sound Zach had ever heard.

Pleasure filled his chest as he watched her look around. "I'm glad you're finally awake."

"I feel like I've been run over. How is Stephanie?"

"She's going to live."

"Will she testify against Carl about how he swindled the company out of almost $100,000?"

Zach smiled at her. "She won't have to. Carl is dead."

She nodded.

"Stephanie told the police that Carl and Ollie paid the field manager to falsify the field reports, and that they stole oil from the tanks and sold it on the open market. The field manager wanted out, and the others didn't want to stop. Someone, either Ollie or Carl—personally I think it was Carl—hit the man on the head with a pipe and tried to make it look like an accident. Ollie must've gotten nervous about the situation, and Carl killed him. The cops ran a ballistics test on the gun Carl shot you with and it matched the one which ended Ollie's life."

"Do you know why Carl decided to swindle the company?" she asked.

"Apparently, he had his sights set on you. When you rejected him, he set out to get revenge."

"What a mess," Toni murmured.

Zach leaned over and lightly kissed her lips. Toni's startled eyes met his.

"Do you remember what I told you in intensive care?" he asked.

"You asked me to fight, for you and the girls."

"That's right because Lisa, Lori and I love you and don't want to lose you."

Her eyes took on a cautious look. "All three of you love me?"

He threaded his fingers through hers. "Yes. I know I once told you that I didn't believe in love. Well, I didn't know what I was talking about. I believe in it now, because I've experienced it. I love you, Toni." His other hand lightly brushed the hair away from her face. "You've shown me the real thing, and taught me to believe. I want this marriage to be the forever-after kind of marriage. What do you say?"

Tears ran into her hair. "You've also taught me something, Zach. That a tough, driven man, like my dad, can also be gentle and tender. You've made a difference in my life. I love you."

Lightly, Zach brushed his lips over hers.

The door opened behind them, and George stood there with both Lisa and Lori.

"Momma," they cried and ran toward the bed.

Zach looked at George. "How'd you get them inside?"

George grinned. "I gave this hospital a lot of money. I simply asked the right folks."

Zach shook his head. Life was going to be interesting.

Epilogue

As they pulled up to the mansion, all of Toni's family was there. They eagerly waited for news of the custody hearing.

Before Zach could turn off the engine, her family rushed out of the house.

"What happened?" J.D. demanded as she threw open the passenger side door.

Toni stood and grinned at the assembled group. "The judge found no reason to terminate Zach's rights as a parent. As far as he could see, Zach is a model father." Pride shone on Toni's face.

"Yeah, the guy in the robe said that we were lucky to have a daddy like ours," Lisa piped in.

"And a momma, too," Lori added.

A round of applause followed. They filed into the house and George poured the champagne. When he tried to hand a glass to Toni, she shook her head.

Everyone gave her an inquiring stare. She poured herself a soft drink, then joined in the toast.

Zach threw her a questioning glance.

"What's going on, daughter?" George asked.

Everyone stared at her. Toni gave up the idea of telling Zach in private. "I'm pregnant and don't want the alcohol."

Stunned surprise greeted her announcement, followed by laughs and hugs.

"How did this happen?" J.D. asked.

Alex shook her head. "The doctors didn't tell Toni it would be impossible, just a slim chance." She turned to Toni. "I believe you beat the chances."

Toni smiled. Finally, Toni was able to turn to Zach. "I hope you're not—"

He put his finger across her lips, stopping her. The love in his heart could clearly be seen on his face. "I'm delighted. Thank you, sweetheart. You've made my life perfect."

She swallowed her tears, and thanked heaven for Zachary Knight with all her heart.

"What's happening?" Lisa demanded.

Toni looked at the twins. "You're going to have a brother or sister in about seven months."

"Really?" Lisa asked, delight on her face.

Toni nodded.

Lisa and Lori looked at each other, then smiled.

"Gee, that's better than having Sam," Lisa commented. "I can't wait."

Zach pulled her close and brushed a kiss across her lips. "This time, I'll get to be there the entire time."

Toni smiled. "You'd better believe it."

* * * * *

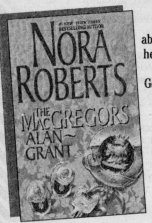
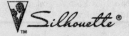

If you enjoyed what you just read,
then we've got an offer you can't resist!

Take 2 bestselling
love stories FREE!

Plus get a FREE surprise gift!

*This March Silhouette
is proud to present*

 Silhouette®

SENSATIONAL

MAGGIE SHAYNE
BARBARA BOSWELL
SUSAN MALLERY
MARIE FERRARELLA

This is a special collection of four complete
novels for one low price, featuring a novel
from each line: Silhouette Intimate Moments,
Silhouette Desire, Silhouette Special Edition
and Silhouette Romance.

Available at your favorite retail outlet.

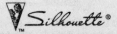 Silhouette®

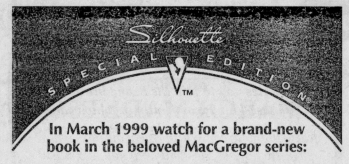

Silhouette

SPECIAL EDITION®

In March 1999 watch for a brand-new book in the beloved MacGregor series:

THE PERFECT NEIGHBOR
(SSE#1232)

by

 # 1 *New York Times* bestselling author

NORA ROBERTS

Brooding loner Preston McQuinn wants nothing more to do with love, until his vivacious neighbor, Cybil Campbell, barges into his secluded life—and his heart.

Also, watch for the MacGregor stories where it all began in the exciting 2-in-1 edition!

Coming in April 1999:

THE MacGREGORS: Daniel—Ian

Available at your favorite retail outlet, only from

Silhouette®